THE COIN

GOPAL O. RANA

First published in 2017 by

Becomeshakespeare.com

Wordit Content Design & Editing Services Pvt Ltd
Unit - 26, Building A -1, Nr Wadala RTO,
Wadala (East), Mumbai 400037, India
T: +91 8080226699
Wordit Art Fund helps deserving authors publish their work by
providing monetary support. To apply for funding, please visit us
atwww.BecomeShakespeare.com

ISBN -978-93-87649-33-0

The Coin

Life is circle of what is our norms and believe. It is not right to say that someone's life is going good or bad. The thing we do is either good or bad but if it helps the other one then it is surely a good deed.

It is 1991. In Gujarat, there is a village called Jhulasan and it is the village which is not so much with facility and have different problem regarding the electricity and other basic problems. Deven matang a boy with not birth like golden spoon on his mouth. After his birth his father was so happy and thought a baby boy came to his house and would solve out the problem of him in future and make them richer at least that size of which can provide them basic easily. His father is simple worker and his name is Rajanbhai matang. He has no farm and he works on daily basis on other's farm and make the money day-wise to feed his family. His mother name is Jhamkhudiben. She is a housewife and also a maid of other's house. After finishing her own house work, she goes to other's house who are richer and ask for work if any. She works for other's house and gets food in exchange of work. She loves her son so much that she can't even like to go outside her house leaving her son. Her house is very small and is made of grass and bamboo not even of bricks, only the wall of little small bricks are there only to support all side of the house so they get lots of problems in rain time and one can say in every season. Parents of Deven are uneducated but his mother is very mature in decision. Once she was on a teacher's house and the teacher is explaining about what we get the benefit if we have less children, that's means less expenses and can teach more to them and etc. She realizes it and ask her husband to have a control as much as he can and use the protection and make a sex after that to have less children so that they can provide at least some education and some needs to their children. Her husband is immature about this and he gets angry with his wife and has an argument about sex. He is the man who is nature- wise not wise so his decisions are most of time dull and he in every time doesn't think of much and uses the money of his earn in only of his family's basic needs with minimum capacity most of time all of whatever he earns. He feels bad about that and he is unable to fill the basic needs even yet. He is the person who is quite disturb with the place he works, he listens there the anger words and abuse of person to whom he works and can't do anything and can't argue there so all the frustration of him he outs to his wife in evening time and his wife is so mature that every time he argues with his wife, she gently handles him kindly.

She believes that "Two side fire only creates fire so one has to be the water in against to the fire. "

It is a evening time and Rajanbhai comes to house from his work, he is tire and not in mood to talk with anybody, he says" What rubbish is this? We poor don't have a life. We are just a wastage of god. We are not capable of doing anything whatever we want? "

His wife asks "What happen to you? always you blame god for anything that happens to you? Are you all right? "

Rajan says in anger "Yes, the god is responsible for everything if anything wrong happens to us. Today I was working and some error occurred on farm and the fucky landlord without any reason blamed me and shouted to me and insulted me. "

She replies" All the people of village know that he is not a good man so everyone has noted who is the right and who is the wrong." and she adds by asking calmly" And what about the good things that has happened to us? "

He shouts extremely" What good has happened to us? are you kidding with me? Tell me what according to you? I don't remember anything. "

She comes to him and replies "God has paired me with you. God has given a handsome husband to me, a nice baby boy to us who has a nice father. "

After listening the praise words, he smiles and says "Yes I am handsome and its very good for you that you get me as your husband. "

Little Deven of 2 year listening the conversation and as he doesn't know anything, he smiles the innocent smile after his mother and father any of them finishes the sentence as he finds the facial expression of his mother and father very funny. His mother sees him and she also smiles so the atmosphere of burning the world goes out and the atmosphere of honey bunny comes to that house.

The child Deven matang is so small so like all the other small babies, he is innocent and very loveable. His father is very frustrate man about the problem being faced by him of money matters and the respect which he wants from the village which he doesn't get so he blames god for it .

Rajanbhai blames god in every morning.

He stands in front of god's picture in his house and says "Hey god I never blame you for my problem in my life and you have given lots of problem to me but I have never complained about this to you but I want to tell you that why are you so much in ignorance of my family that you never see at us and our problem. "

He is cool till now but after this his temperament goes high and out of his mind and says" In real you don't want to see to me. You never understand my problem what I am going through. Every morning I am thinking about night that am I able to bring food to my family this night or we have to sleep without any food . You are responsible for this and you have to do something otherwise I will understand that you are always only for rich people and not for people like us."

After this his frustration goes on high and his voice goes little high "What are you doing god? Do me a favor and either kill me or feed us. Solve our problem or free us from all the problem and take us to your house so that I can personally talk with you that what wrong I have done so that you are punishing me like this? "

His frustration goes on to the cloud nine and he shouts to his wife "Why you have put this god to our house? he is not our ,he is only of rich people and he is never going to listen to our problem. I am going to throw this god out of my house and never want him to get back as he never ever try any solution to us. "

His wife is listening all this and as she is very much of patience person and she knows her husband personality very much and also she knows that every morning he does that and it is not new of him,

She replies calmly "Do you really want to throw god out of our house then I am not going to stop you." thinking slightly and adds "In real, you are right, God never going to listen to us . He is not our cup of tea and we are not his cup of tea so we are not going to be listened by him and not you but this time I am going to throw him out of my house. "

After replying to her husband, she goes near her husband where the photo of god is put. She looks at her husband and slowly slowly takes her hand to god's photo as if she were going to throw god's photo out of the house.

Her husband stops her hand and asks her in anger "Are you crazy? Is this a joke? " his wife replies "You just told me that you want to throw the god out of our house so I am just helping you nothing else."

Her husband says "Yah! I was saying that but that doesn't mean really that I am in real wanting that I want to throw god out of our house in real. "

She knows that he is now in control so creating the atmosphere light in an acting manner with surprise, she says " Oh! You want to fear god that you are going to throw him out of your house so that in fear of that god will solve your problem as early as possible. "

He now understands what she is trying to say but he is staring at her so his wife adds again in her acting manner so with delight " You are very clever. Every time god fears us of doing bad to us and also that he is going to punish us if we will do anything wrong about the good manners that given to us by him so he can punish us and you are fearing him about to get out him from his one of the house out of many houses in world so he gets fear and help us as early as possible. "

He smiles and takes his hand to his head and rubbing his hair replies " O.k, o.k I know what you want to say to me," After saying that in smile, he faces his face to little anger and says " Don't do like this to me again otherwise god being thrown or not ,you are going to be beaten by me. "

She replies calmly again in acting manner "As you want my god husband. " and hugs him tightly.

That's the manner every morning Rajanbhai complaints to god in slightly different manner and that's the manner every morning Jhamkhudiben replies to him. As the complaints of Rajanbhai changes, the replies of Jhamkhudiben changes but every time Jhamkhudiben convinces him by her answer and every time Rajanbhai got convinced by her.

As the time travels, Deven becomes three year old as his mother is doing household job to some rich people house. She can't put the boy in house alone. Till Deven is three year old she gave her son to her neighbor for take care. One day the neighbor where she puts her son says "I am tire of caring your son and I have also my son and daughters so taking care of that much children is not possible for me so please take your son with you and forgive me please. "

Jhamkhudiben replies like always with polite "O.k don't worry and it is nice that you have told me your problem and as you are getting tire of this and I can understand this. From tomorrow I will take my son with me." from that day she always takes her son with her wherever she goes. She is working on three different people houses. One is a teacher who has two daughters and his wife died after giving birth to second daughter as he has no wife, Jhamkhudiben goes there for only cooking food and for this she doesn't charge anything but takes a promise that the master is going to teach her son free or on little cost when her son will get older of that age of studying. The other one is land lord of that village and they are of high caste too so she is not allowed to touch anything from kitchen even so she goes there for cleaning the house. The third one where she goes is the house of a merchant where she goes for the work of both cooking and cleaning for which she gets not money but food items. The merchant lives in city and he does all his transaction in city and just to meet his relatives, he comes there and nothing else.

The relatives live in his house and they are there to get the benefit of jhamkhudiben freely as the merchant pays to her. So Jhamkhudiben has no free time till evening and after all this, she goes to own house and makes meal for her family. She never complaints about this to anyone as she wants her son to learn more and break the barrier of poorness so her son won't do that type of struggle that she and her husband has done and got nothing for that.

One day when working on the house of landlord, she is cleaning the house and finds one gold ear ring which she urgently takes with her to the landlord and tells him " Sir ,I have found one gold ear ring while cleaning the house. "

The landlord very soon snatches that ear ring from her hand and says "good, "

After thinking some second, he asks her "This is the only one and where is the second one? "

She replies "Sir I have found only one and I immediately bring that to you. I don't know about the second one. "

The landlord asks "Do you think I am fool ? Yesterday my wife lost both of her ear rings at night time and you are saying that you found only one , how is it possible? "

She replies "Sir what is true that is I am telling to you and nothing else sir.",

"I have worked here for many years and such things I have found many of times and every time I have immediately returned to either you or madam . " She adds,

The landlord starts the argument and as he knows that she is poor and under him so shouts again "You have returned every time honestly but this time you are cheating with us as I have heard that you and your family often sleep without eating and going through lots of problem, so this time may be you are lying and cheating with us. "

She replies "Sir you have heard this only this time and me and my family are facing the problem of meal and basic problem from many years, so there is no question of lying to you or taking any of your ornaments with me. "

The landlord realizes that she is saying true and she is honest but the ego of landlord is being hurt as not many of time one can argue with him and in little time of argument in that time, she has won over him, that's what he feels.

He calls his wife "Hey, darling come here. "

His wife replies "What happened? "

He tells "Jhamkhudi has found one of your two ear rings. "

His wife replies" Oh really! "

She starts running immediately to her husband and says "Thank you Jhamkhudi for this. "

The landlord says "That's o.k but I have doubt that Jhamkhudi has found the other one also but she is lying to us that she has found only one. "

Jhamkhudi is there and with the innocent eyes. She looks at her madam as if she is asking that madam, can I do like this ever?

His wife replies "No, no darling , it is not possible . She is very honest and I have full trust on her. Every time she has found anything , she has returned even costlier than this ear ring to me so there is no question of doubting on her. "

The ego of the landlord hurts high by that reply of his wife as he thinks that his wife has trust her more than him and shouts to his wife "You don't understand anything , you are fool and she is taking advantage of your stupidity. "

Little Deven is little far away and seeing all these and he understands nothing what is going on and why the person is shouting on his mother. As all other little baby would do at that point of time, he also does same thing at that point and starts crying.

As Deven starts crying, his mother goes to him and starts loving him and says "Nothing my son, nothing has happened, you please stop crying. "

The landlord's wife tells to her husband" You are for no reason doubting on her, please stop this. "

The landlord replies by making his face with different expression " You just shut your mouth up and keep quiet. I know what I am doing and don't interfere about this otherwise you are going to be beaten up by me and you know how I beat so you decide what you want."

His wife knows him and knows she is going to get punished if after this she is going to favor Jhamkhudi so she goes to Jhamkhudi and says " Sorry but I can't help you . Please forgive me and manage by yourself. "

Jhamkhudi goes upset and replies "That's O.k madam, I will try . I don't want that you are being beaten for favoring me. "

The very next second landlord orders "All the servants come here."

All servants present there in little time and after this he adds "You all lady servant take jhamkhudi in side that room and take off all her clothes and make her naked and check everything carefully either she has taken ear ring or not? "

All the servants are looking at each other and asks "How can this done by us sir? she is honest and it is insult of her if we are going to do like this to her. "

The landlord in his thinking with happiness says to own self " Yes that insult I want of her as she has hurt my ego. "

The landlord replies " If you are not going to do this then I will fire all of you and you know that there are lots of workers who are ready to work here. "

All the lady servants have no other option and have to do that. They go near to Jhamkhudi and tell to her "Sorry, but we have no other option than doing this. "

Normally Jhamkhudi is tough but this time she cries and tells the landlord "Please don't do this to me . I have done nothing wrong sir."

All the lady servants take her to room and they take off her all clothes and start searching for that ear ring. At that time Jhamkhudi is crying very much, her tears are unstoppable. No one has ever seen her crying like this ever. On outside, the landlord is hearing the weeping noise of her and he is very happy for that.

After some time all servants come out and tell "Nothing is with her."

The ego of landlord is now satisfied by the revenge he thinks and replies" O.k now I am satisfied that she has not taken my wife's ear ring and she can start her work again. All of you can start also. "

All are going to their work, all of sudden Jhamkhudi shouts and says with tears "Sir everyone knows that I can't do that, even you know but just for your ego, you have done this to me . Now I am not going to work here anymore but I want to say that time changes to everyone and you are not out of this world. "Saying this she takes her son and starts going out of the landlord's house.

All servants are looking at her and the landlord feels sorry but as he is landlord so he doesn't stop her. Jhamkhudi is crying and walking towards her house and all the village people who are seeing her, start whispering what has happened so for the first time she is crying like this. She is carrying Deven and walking. Deven is looking at his mother and cleaning his mother's tear from her chick with his little hand and also looking at the people who are looking at his mother with different manner. Slowly slowly this incidence goes to the ear of every person of village. Everybody is talking about Jhamkhudi in village. Like all, this goes to Rajan also. He immediately takes a leave from his work and runs towards his house. In house Jhamkhudi is crying so also Deven is crying. Rajan runs till his house not come and suddenly he stops at the door. He is looking at his wife and son and both are crying. He has seen first time Jhamkhudi crying like this so he goes emotional also and he also cries. He slowly goes to his wife and firstly he gives water to her. As he is also crying so Jhamkhudi realizes that somehow the incident must have listened by him also. The house is very very silent and only tears are coming out of their eyes . They both are looking at each other's eyes and their eyes are showing the weakness of their and heart beat are high of both. In that time, their mutual understanding are going so pure that they even don't need words to say to each other. Jhamkhudi knows that her husband loves her so much but for the first time she sees that her husband is showing his love to her with that much of care. Rajan comes to her and sits near to her and puts his hand on her chick to clean her tears and at same time, his wife is doing same with him .He hugs her slowly. He then takes her head to his palm like a little baby and slowly slowly starts handing his hand in her head. The whole half day and night goes like that. In this whole incidence, for the First time Rajan has shown how much he loves to Jhamkhudi so that he feels her pain like that the pain of jhamkhudi is not only of her but his also.

One year later, Deven is four year old so his mother is taking him to school for junior kg. Jhamkhudi's only wish is one day her son will get education of high so that he can earn money and will not have to suffer like she and her husband have.

She is taking her son to master for the first time so Deven is crying and she is advising "Education is only way we can get out of our poorness and you must study very carefully.

I know you are so small to understand this but you have to understand it and as early you understand it that is good for you and us. "

Then Deven asks "What is the connection between poorness and education? Is every literate is rich? "

She replies "No connection, it is possible that the person who is literate he may be is poor. "

Deven again asks" So why are you saying that I have to study more to finish our poorness? "

She replies "Poorness is may be possible for literate person but now days education is the only way by which one can get more knowledge. How to take the nice path in life. It teaches you the freedom of life, it teaches you to not to be feared of anyone and it teaches you the value of valuable things and how to create the value of that thing which has no value and the last one is education means opportunity which you have to cash on. "

Deven asks again "As everyone knows that you are not literate then how you know all this, mother?"

She replies " This is common my boy and everybody knows now days this and for extra I have learned that you think is the lesson that I have learned in house of your master while working there."

Deven says "Oh! Now I understand. " after walking few more steps, he adds " Don't worry mom I am going to study very carefully and one day I will finish our poorness. "

She replies "That is expected from you and always try to learn more. "

Deven answers "O.k mom I will. "

Talking is going on and they reach the school. In school master is teaching and he welcomes Deven as his mother has already talked with him of his admission the day before today. Master is very kind and he teaches his students as if the students were his own sons and daughters. In village his respect is more than any person. He teaches them not only the lessons of book but also the good and the bad thing of life that are going to teach them for the survival of life and how to face the challenges. The village's school is not with so much facility so there are no benches in every class and some class students have to sit on floor .Deven sits on floor and Master is in front of all the students,

"All the boys first of all please welcome our new student Deven matang. " Master says to everybody.

All students in one voice cheers " Welcome Deven. "

The master says "Deven as I know your mom, she has not studied but she is very intelligent and mature and always ready to learn new things in life. I hope you are like your mother and make her proud to you one day by getting the success that your mother wants from you. I hope that."

"I will try sir." answers Deven,

Then sir starts his lesson from basics, sir is teaching and asking to everybody "Do all of you understand? "

All students replies "Yes sir, Yes sir. "

Deven also mixes his voice in all of them but in real Deven understands very little.

Sir asks to everyone "If anyone has any question or doubt about that what i have taught you then without any hesitation ask me about the matter or question and i will answer all yours doubt. By asking questions you are going to clear your doubt and that will increase your understanding power. "

But Deven shows hesitation in asking and never asks any question in that day. Sir has understood it and he knows that on day first, one can't understand very much and it is quite common but he does not forced Deven for asking questions because he knows that if by forcing Deven, may be he will ask the question but how long that may go so he wants him to ask question by his own self not by any force. In all the time of class Deven does nothing. Some time he is seeing outside the class, sometime he is enjoying with friends, even sometime he goes sleep for minutes and finally if sometime remains he passes in study but without care. Sir has noticed that he is not showing interest on study and very much dull but because it is first day of him so he remains silent in that day. Finally the last ring rings out and all the students start their running towards their house so as Deven. Deven after the final ring feels very happy that finally he is going out of school and starts his running but all of sudden master calls " Deven , come here."

Deven stops there and thinks "What is going on and why is sir now calling me? Am I have done anything wrong, is sir going to punish me, what may be reason? "

Thinking all this, he starts his walk towards his master .His face is showing lots of questions.

Deven reaches to master and asks " Yes sir ,what happened ? Am I have done anything wrong sir? "

The master very calmly puts his hand on his shoulder and replies " First of all relax my boy. "

Deven starts feeling good and his questions fly away.

The master asks him "Today In class, Do you have understood everything that I have taught to you? " in his voice the master is asking more like friend than the teacher.

Deven firstly thinks something and after very little time replies "Not in real sir ji. Today in class whatever you have taught to me that goes bounce of me and I felt much time bore . Sometime I thought of even running out of class but my mother's lessons have stopped me so I by force stay there and have bear you sir. "

After hearing the answer of Deven sir starts to laugh " Then what happened when I have told everyone if they have any question or have any doubt ,they can ask me without any hesitation? "sir again asks friendly.

Deven replies " Sir first think first ,I understood very little today and some questions have arisen in my mind but haven't asked ,I don't know the reason why I haven't asked in spite of your very kindly mention about the doubts. "

Sir thinks for some seconds and says" O.k you may go but always remember that I am like your friend and you can ask me any question anytime and I will definitely help you. "

" O.k sir " replies Deven and starts his running towards his house.

The master can have punished him or threaten him for his misbehaving attitude but he hasn't because master feels that Deven can study anytime the lesson of chapter but once if he has told the answer by making on his own self and if he has told lie to him then that can be very dangerous and it may create problem to his goodness. The master is very happy that his student has told him the truth so he leaves him without any punishment or threat.

Deven reaches his house and directly hugs his mother "Mom I really miss you in school " says Deven.

His mother also hugs him" Oh really! The school is not much time far from our house and you are there for some hours and you have missed me?" she says it in that manner like she was also a child.

" Yes very much " says Deven.

"My brave boy , what you have learned in school today?" she asked very kindly .

Deven replies " Very few things."

His mother asks him with surprise " Why ? Anything wrong happened there to you, my boy? "

Deven replies "No mom but in real most of lesson goes bounce of my head, that's why I am saying that I have learned very few things in school."

His mother has never gone for school but with her life experience, she knows that everything in this world takes time for learning so she says " O.k my boy ,whatever you have learned today that's good but tomorrow try to learn more than today, my good boy, won't you? "

"yes I will," he replies .

After few months in the morning time Rajan is working his work and preparing to go for his work. Jhamkhudi is also working her household work and Deven is playing outside his house and suddenly Jhamkhudi feels little uncomfortable and dizziness. She starts running towards outside. Rajan sees this and he also runs after his wife .In outside Jhamkhudi is vomiting.

Deven is already there so he asks " What happened mom, why are you vomiting? Are you all right mom?"

Jhamkhudi replies " Nothing my boy."

Rajan reaches there and he also repeats the question same of Deven . Firstly she smiles and remains silent and shies by looking at her husband eyes.

"Why are you smiling and not answering to my question?" he asks in very surprise manner,

She again feels shy and runs in to house. Rajan and his son also walks inside house.

"Can you please tell me what is all happening? " he asks,

"I am not understanding what is going on ?" he adds ,

"I am expecting. " she replies in very slow voice ,

"What? I don't get you. Please repeat but this time in loud voice. " he says,

She comes to him and slightly whispers "I am expecting. "

This time Rajan hears the sentence.

" Really ?" he asks her with very happy gesture .

She replies "Yes. "

He immediately hugs his wife and loud his voice" yes, yes I will be a father again. "

Deven stands near to him, he is very confuse and asks in same gesture " Can any one of you please state what is going on and why you both are happy so much?"

Rajan and his wife sees him and smiles,

"My son you will be a brother, the elder brother." replies Rajan,

Deven hasn't understood clearly but his ear has heard that he will become brother means he will become something so he also joins them and hugs both of them and makes his voice on commanding position "mom I will become something and something will happen happily so I will get something and something may come to me for which you both will be happy " says Deven.

Firstly Deven hasn't understood all clearly and this time both of them haven't understood what Deven in real wants to say but they all are happy. It is like from years there is no happiness in that house which is suffering from the dryness of happiness. Deven starts his round around his mother and father and runs out of the house in cheering manner. He is dancing ,singing and repeats his sentence again and again and starts his round to village. Everybody has started asking to Deven what has happened and Deven replies how his mother has vomited and mother and father went inside house and what his father had replied to him . So like this the news of his mother pregnancy circulated all around the village. People starts coming to Rajan's house and everybody congratulates Jhamkhudi for her expecting. In meanwhile while all whoever has come and congratulated deven's mother,

Deven is thinking " Mom is becoming something ,father is becoming something and lastly I am also becoming something so why all the people from village are coming in my house and congratulating my mom? Are all the people of village also becoming something so they all are also happy? "

This is the very emotional moment of Jhamkhudi's house . She and her family are so poor and in poor's house happy moment comes rarely and the house where the family members have to struggle for their food and basic thing, this is like event so in evening time by borrowing some money from others, Rajan goes in shop and asks " Brother ,please give me 1 kg basmati rice,1 packet butter and 1 kg red kidney beans ."

He takes all the things and goes to his house early from all the previous days. He then gives that all the items to his wife and asks her to cook all these things that night .

He happily makes his word" Today I am so happy and I want you both also to be happy."

She replies "We are also happy and I am so much wonder about your happiness. After so long time I have seen you happy this much so now my happiness has no limit. "

She then takes all the things and goes for cooking.

In eating time, Deven says "Mom tonight our food are different from all others days and is very tasty . I wish we were to have to eat these types of food daily."

His mother replies " I am sure that that day will come surly one day ,for now don't think so much about this and silently with peaceful mind eat it and let us also enjoy it my boy."

"O.k mom " he replies.

After eating food and working all household work, Jhamkhudi comes to bed. Their bed are of one of fat cloth on floor. Deven is sleeping and Jhamkhudi's husband is waiting for her .She slowly comes to him and stands near to him. Rajan is sitting on floor bed .

He says "I love you so much. Without you my life is empty glass ,you are the one without whom I can't leave without even for a second. You are my soul and you are the only one who has taught me my value of life ,living standard. Over all, you are the circle of me in which I want to circulate and I want nothing. "

Saying this he touches her feet.

" What are you doing, In our religion husband never touches the feet of his wife, it is sin " she says in hesitation .

He again touches the feet then says " Please don't stop me, nothing is sin. When wife has to touch the feet of husband then husband can also touch his wife's feet. I am touching it because of your personality, your value, your goodness, your qualities and all other thing that I realize about you have. "

His wife also sits with him and she says "You are praising so much, you are my love and you are also soul of me. "

She sees in his eyes and finds the romance,

She includes "Today why are you much romantic? "

He answers" You are always love of me. I am always romantic to you but till now I have never revealed it with you but today my happiness has broken all the barriers of myself and whatever I have felt that I have told to you. "

Then he touches her hand, kisses on hand and hugs her so tightly. Jhamkhudi also starts to feel him, he then kisses her on her stomach and slowly slowly the kiss goes up side her body. All the atmosphere goes romantic with mood. Jhamkhudi also starts to kiss him first on his head then on his chick. He kisses her on her neck and starts biting her ear. Both bodies are feeling full on sex, he then kisses her on her lips. Both are on heaven and all night goes with romance and sex.

Seven and half month later in night time Jhamkhudi starts her labour pain .

" I think time has come ,please go to Rekhaben's house and ask her to come here as early as possible." Says jhamkhudi,

Rekhaben is the women who helps women of village to have a child at the time of delivery. She is the woman who has experience of it from last 45 years as her mom had done same kind of work in the village. Her age is about 65 and she is the one to whom everyone goes for that work. Hospitals are far away from village and the cost of Rekhaben's work is nothing, just have to give something for the happiness which she makes to the couple. Rajan immediately runs towards Rekhaben's house for the help. Here the pain of Jhamkhudi increases .Rajan runs and reaches the house of Rekhaben. He knocks the door of her and her daughter in law opens the door.

"Where is Rekhaben? " he asks,

She replies "She is sleeping. "

He in hurry says "I need her immediate. My wife delivery pain has started, please wake up her and say about this. "

She goes inside house and says "Mother in law wake up please. Jhamkhudi 's pain has started and she is calling you. Her husband has arrived here to take you with him. "

Her mother in law wakes up slowly and comes outside the house. They are walking towards Rajan's house.

She asks " When the pain has begun? "

He answers "Approx 15 to 20 minute before. "

She again asks " Is she o.k ?"

He replies "When she felt about her pain was increasing, she immediately ask me to call you. "

She says "Don't worry this is just a beginning and child comes not just like that. It is a process and it will take time , I just have to help her else she has to do own self. "

In her words, words clearly have shown her experience and she is very calm. She knows this is common and happens to everyone. By her words Rajan also feels some relax full .They reach to his house . Rajan takes Deven out of house and Rekhaben locks the door from inside. Firstly she starts bowling water and takes clothes to rub her. Jhamkhudi has also experience of delivery at the time of Deven so she is also in patience and following all the instruction of Rekhaben .The pain of her starts rising and She is pressuring the child to come out of her . Rekhaeben is pushing the child slowly in her stomach and motivating her while the pain rises . Inside the house they are calm and processing their own work but outside the house Rajanbhai is nervous and goes hyper as the sound of his wife's pain comes out. After sometime from inside the house, little child 's crying voice comes out . Rajan knows what that is mean of and feels happy.

Rekhaben comes out of the house and says "Congratulation the goddess of money now on earth, she is in your house. "

Rajan is very happy and his emotions are out of control. Deven is also there and is confuse about what She has told ,thinking that goddess has come in my house , how is it possible ? Goddess live on heaven and my home is like hell of dryness of everything , so how can this be possible?

Deven asks to his father "Goddess has come to our house, how this is possible father? "

His father replies "Baby girl child is symbol of goddess Lakshmi so it is the saying whenever girl child delivered that goddess of money has arrived. "

Rajan in happiness gives Rekhaben his some vessels and one old sari to her and Rekhaben leaves the house happily by instruction of lots of care to new born child as it is mandatory. After some seconds, he goes inside, he goes near to his wife. She is lying on bed and her child is near to her, she is taking care of her. He sits near to them, slowly slowly touches his child. Deven also comes there and after seeing his sister

"Wow! Mom, she is very cute. " says deven,

Tears are coming out of both Rajan and his wife's eyes slowly slowly. Looking at each other by eyes they are showing their emotions and happiness.

Rajan says "I am very happy ,I am sure she will change our luck one day as she is our luck. "

Jhamkhudi adds" Yes she will, she is very loveable. "

"Loveable, yes she is loveable so we will call her PRIYA the one who is loveable to everyone. Isn't this good name to her ?" Rajan says.

Deven says in excitement "Wow! What a beautiful name!, yes we will call her Priya, loveable to everyone, "

After few seconds Deven adds "Priya, my sister name is very sweet ,Priya has arrived, Priya has arrived, she is cute ."

The night is happiest of their life.

Some days later Rajan is on school for Deven's report card.

Rajan asks "I can't understand much so please tell me what this report card shows and how he is on his study? "

Master replies "Very poor, he is very poor on his study . He has no care about his study. He is good boy and honest but is not so good in his study. His hard work is brilliant but overall is low in his study. "

Rajan says " I am also tense about him. I have also seen his careless in study and lots of time he is on his playing way and I have asked about the study then totally ignores my questions and runs away from there." without understanding the report card , he looks at that,

"Please suggest us what we should do about his study?" Rajan asks kindly.

Master replies " I have also tried lots of time that Deven must has to focus more about his study but his attention is on his study never increases, but In all this, I have seen one more thing that his smart work on life has increases more than his study . Many of times his answers are beyond the catch of me even, his attention towards money is like he is only to earn, he has just one thing in his mind that is how to earn more money. In short, study is not his cup of tea ,his only aim is money and the main point is yet he is honest and always speaks true. "

Rajan says" Just thinking about money if that can give us money then I also were on list of millionaire but just thinking never gives anyone bread so I will punish him today and will make to pay attention only to his study. "

Master laughs in his manner and replies" If by forcing to study, child can pay attention on study more than then definitely in india everyone would have become doctor, engineer, ca, and other well qualified degrees and studies but this is not right. People have their own mentality ,yah! I know hardness is sometime mandatory to some student but Deven is not one of them. If I am right For Deven, sky is not going to be the limit just because of one thing that is his honesty and fearless about everything."

Listening to this facial expression of Rajan becomes freak.

Master adds "yah! you hear it right, a person who is fearless can do anything. Fear creates hurdle to our life and if persons fear of then he will be one always under his fear and target goes out of his reach. Deven is god gifted boy who has fear of nothing so be calm and let the time decide everything."

Rajan replies "I don't understand much but I will do as you have told, I will follow your advice."

Master says" Take this report card and leave this matter and tell me about your work, how's that going on ?"

Rajan replies in very upset mood "What to say about work, some day there is work and some days there is not. When there is work that day is good but when there is not then we have to suffer from dryness of money and we have to adjust by borrowing money from others . Like this I am passing my days and suffering. "

Master asks" How long you will do like this? , you have to do something. "

"What can I do sir, nothing is on my hand. " replies Rajan,

Master advises " You can. Take some money from me and open a little small shop and pay attention to that. Surely you will get success and your problem will also be solved out by this."

Rajan asks " How can I take money from you? It is my responsibility to give you money, I have failed on that. Now you are asking me to take money from you, it is not possible sir."

Master asks him" let me teach you, you are one person and I am also. I am helping you because you are honest and I have full trust on you."

"That's o.k sir but what will happen if I will fail on shop and will not able to return your money. "rajan asks his common sense question,

Master replies "Think positive, you have to take it and do a hard work nothing else, if not then I will go angry with you."

Firstly Rajan rejects to accept that money but by in force of master Rajan takes money and after some days he starts his own shop. Rajan feels the luck of his daughter, he feels that after the entrance of his daughter this shop has started so he loves her lot and takes care of her more than Deven. Rajan often ignores deven. Deven often feels bad about this but his mother takes that situation on right way and she loves both of them equal. She often tries to say Rajan about this but Rajan totally ignores this .She only can do is to support Deven .Slowly slowly by the time, the difference between

Rajan and Deven rises. Often Deven tries to talk with his father but Rajan replies in very short and ignores him after that. The talk of both of them now is very less but sometime Rajan talks with Deven by only the instruction of jhamkhudi. jhamkhudi is now the bridge between them , she takes care of both of them and the issue of luck which Rajan feels about his daughter Priya , She handles that very well.

As the time rolls on, Priya is now of three year old. She is sweet baby, she is the charm of village. Everybody in the village loves her because of her cuteness. In the small age of three, her intelligence has impressed everyone. Her naughty thinks are also charm of her. Nobody in the village dislikes her, even the person is fret of little small child that types of person also loves her. In village whoever comes near the house of Rajan , they come inside house of Rajan just to see Priya. Sometimes if there is nobody in the house then Priya stops everyone and says with her small tongue, with her small hand, whenever she says anything, her hand expression is the centre of attraction to everyone and in her cute sweet voice says " What you want ?"

If woman is in front of her then woman replies "Where is Jhamkhudi? I have some work with her."

"She is not at home, What is the work? you can tell me that." Priya asks,

 The woman answers "No, no, I have work with your mother, the matter is high, you can't understand it. "

Priya makes heavy voice and the cuteness is always there with her and says" There is nothing in this world which I can't do.

In absence of my mother and father, I am the handler of this house and everything is possible for me, you understand it aunty. "

The woman smiles and is very happy about the cute answers that Priya has given . She is impressed with her like everyone in the village, she says "o.k my little baby, I will come after some time . This is a chocolate , take it. "

Like this Priya answers everyone's questions. Sometime people know that there is nobody in the house else than Priya but just to listen her cute voice, her wordings, her smartness, her sharpness ,to see her naughty things, people goes to Rajan's house and everybody returns from there with smile on their face. One day in night time everybody is waiting for dinner, Deven is singing song and waiting. Priya is playing with her toys and waiting. Rajan is calculating his shop's work and waiting. After sometime when Jhamkhudi finishes her cooking, she calls everyone to wash their hand and come to eat. Everybody immediately washes hand and runs for the food. Jhamkhudi is serving food to everyone, as per size she first serves to her husband in big plate more khichdi, millet bread and more vegetable. Then she serves to Deven in smaller than Rajan's plate less than Rajan's khichdi, millet bread and less vegetable to him. Then the turn is of Priya, in a small plate as she is just three year old and can't eat much, she gives her little khichdi, small piece of millet bread and very less vegetable. Everybody starts eating their meal, Jhamkhudi also starts her meal. Everybody else than Priya starts eating. Everybody is looking at her why she is not eating her meal. Priya is miffed with everyone, she puts her both hand in her palm and looks to everyone with anger.

Her mother asks her "What happen to you? "

Priya turns around and does not reply of her mother's question. Rajan also asks the same question but same response comes from priya. Rajan gets tense what would have happened because of which she is not eating her meal. Jhamkhudi sees to her husband and his preoccupation. She slowly raises her hand and in sign language signs that don't worry about her, I will handle everything.

She goes to Priya and puts her hand on her head by rounding her hand with lots of love she asks" Why are you not eating your meal my sweet baby, tell me? "

Priya replies in very innocence " I everyday see that you serve that's so little to everybody and that so much to me . Go I will not eat , go I will not eat, this is injustice. "

Everybody in house laughs, they know what priya is trying to say so little to her and much more to everybody else but due to her childness innocence and less knowledge, she is saying opposite of that.

Jhamkhudi then replies "Oh! That's the problem of my baby. Sorry baby, I will provide you more, come and eat it. "

Jhamkhudi then acts of taking khichdi from vessel and acts of putting on her plate same with vegetables also. Then the miffness of Priya goes down and she also starts to eat her meal. This type of incidence often takes place in Rajan's house and every time Priya shows her innocence and intelligence. Everybody in village knows Jhamkhudi so all start saying that priya is like her mother. "Like mother like daughter " people are saying it. Some people even are saying that Priya is brilliant than her mother. On her little age as all know that this not time for her school but she wishes with her family for school. Rajan talks with master and gets her daughter admission. She is of book girl, she likes reading ,studying is now becomes her soul. Everybody and all the people of village are surprise with her hobby of learning. Master is proud of her.

On other side in Ahmedabd, there lives a family of Patel. Head of family is Maheshbhai patel, his wife Neha and they have one son and his name is Vivek. Vivek is six year old. Maheshbhai is billionaries, he has many house in many state of india but he loves to live in Ahmedabad as his connection with Ahmedabad is deeper. He has lots of industries all over india. Recently forbes magazine has released their list of world's top 100 richest person of year and in that list Maheshbhai is on first number. They have no depletion of anything. Vivek studies on top most school of ahmedabad. Thing which he demands for that will come to him even before an hour. Their life is of king size. Vivek is very enjoyable boy, he enjoys everything very well. There house is like palaces, where there are lots of servants and lots of maid for their meal cooking and for other work and to do household work of house. Everyone is of expertise of his or her own work and for that one is getting high salary than one common man can imagine. That is all about the only system of work of Maheshbhai's house servants. Maheshbhai has lots of industry, textile industry, chemical industry, engineering and etc. etc. Maheshbhai's family are rich from their forefathers. All the business of Maheshbhai was started by his grandfather at the time of British empire on india. His grandfather had started first of all in british rule in india a firm of textile which he had name that THE PATEL TEXTILE so after that textile, all the firm which he had started were also in name of Patel so the rules continues till now and whenever Maheshbhai starts his new venture, he also names his industry THE PATEL with the following thing that of he wants to open. In india there are very few things which is not in business of Maheshbhai. From milk ,bread , ac ,cars, cement ,steel ,chemicals ,the real estate business, cold drinks ,food items, The shoping mall, all the electronics items, the control of education system including the education sector business. There are lots of colleges in india in which trusty is Maheshbhai . Maheshbhai has that much of money which one common man can't think of .Maheshbhai often travels all around the world, there is almost no country in this world which is not visited by him. His one minute is like million rupees, so he doesn't have time for anything. He in family loves his son Vivek more than anyone. May be the reason behind his love is that he is the only son of him and he can never see tears on his son eyes so whatever his son demands for, that he presents just like that. In Vivek's birthday in one snap he calls for big celebrity whoever his son demands for and by his calling, no one can refuse because of his power in india. In india he is the number one richest person and above the richest list of india so he has connection with politicians even with prime minister his connection is like brother. In other words the policies of india about the economics decision which are taken by the minister are in advised of Maheshbhai. Common people don't know about this but this is the fact and every economist knows this but no one is in position to raise his voice against this. Due to this many of times, he has changed for his business benefit the economic policies of India from the back door of committee. He doesn't care about the benefit of common people but like all the business man, he only wants his profit to increase nothing matters else than that to him. The only weakness of Maheshbhai is over the limit believing in god. He is very superstitious, his trust on god is more than himself. In every month, one or two day is fix for him to visit god temple. This schedule is fixed by himself and he is such a person that in time of his visit to temple if any emergency comes out then he leaves that emergency and goes for temple visit. Sometimes due to his superstitious nature, his wife and his son and even the staff members of his office suffers many of problem. His son say of being in problem due to that his norms and the staff members have to adjust according to his believe but from behind the staff members only say bed words to him and the weakness of maheshbhai.

Vivek's mother Neha is originally not Gujarati. She is from West Bangal. Her birth place was Kolkata and her name was Neha basu. She had studied in London with the degree of M.B.A. Her father was also a businessman. At one of party of high society, the father of Maheshbhai and the father of Neha had met and during the discussion of business they decided to joint their business. The amalgamation process they were discussing and after the discussion they both came to know about the each other's family and they decided the marriage between the Maheshbhai and neha . Neha was very beautiful and didn't want to marry Mahesh because of her love to other boy but due to the pressure of family, she was forced to marry with Mahesh. Neha had no option but only had to marry Mahesh. She had agreed herself by force for marriage. The marriage happened and after some years after the birth of Vivek , Mahesh came to know that before marriage Neha had a boyfriend and she was serious about him but by force only she had agreed for the marriage. Mahesh argued with his wife about that. Neha had many of time explained to Mahesh that her boy boyfriend was her past and he is her present and after marriage she hadn't met his boyfriend ever and now the world of Neha was only Mahesh and her son Vivek but Maheshbhai didn't want to understand it. He was doubting his wife and for that they had big argument many of times with each other. One night in bedroom Neha asked about that how long he was going for that type of doubt and the argument to talk with her. The argument increased, Neha was explaining and Mahesh was not ready to understand so in mid of that big argument, Mahesh slept her and after that Neha was beaten by belt and other things very dreadfully. From that night they don't talk with each other. They hadn't gone for divorce just because of their son Vivek because they both love Vivek very much. Maheshbhai was not divorcing her because he knew that if the divorce matter went on in court, his son is very small so the court would give his son to his wife and he had to live life separate from his son and In other side, Neha was not ready for divorce because she knew that she was innocent and if she divorced with him, his doubt went on strong and after marriage her husband and her son was the world of her. She had a believed that one day Mahesh would realize the truth but after beaten up by her husband, her moral went down and just for her son, she lived with Mahesh. So Maheshbhai and Neha from that day have not their argument every day but the silent cold war started. After some time Neha also lost her patience and she also started to not to talk with her husband. Neha is a good mother ,she takes care of her son very smartly with so much love .After that fight she has started an NGO for the girl who are victims of heart cracking incidence. The NGO is for that types of women and little baby for whom there is no reason to live life. Some women who are in prostitution profession by force and if they want to leave that and wants help from Neha then she is the one who helps them and teach them to live life by forgetting their past life . For that she has started cottage industry where every girl who are brought from, who are victims of people and the girl who are molested by the society for their self respect. They work there and live their life. Neha is the woman who stimulus every woman to be self respective about them self. She teaches every girl to be independent and their life has not finished, their life has just started and they have to show their power all over the world. They can live their life as they want .Nobody else than Vivek knows that his mother and his father doesn't talk with each other . In society they behave like they are good couple and they are very happy with each other and that is by even without talking to each other and that is the hardest thing with both of them as you are showing happiness to other and that is without talking to your partner and that is very hard and sometime goes wrong even. This is bitter truth of this society that Neha who motivates every girl of her NGO about the independence of women and their right to live their life as they want ,from inside Neha is broken heart woman whose husband had doubted about her character and is living with her husband just because of her son . Often when she teaches the women of NGO about the importance of independence, she realizes that her life is not even independent. She was forced by her emotion to live with her husband. After Starting her NGO, she gives all the time to The NGO and her son. She is always ready for help of any women and also for her son to whom she loves more than her life.

Vivek is on the way to become six year old and his parents love him very much. He is the boy who has taken birth with golden spoon in his mouth .His father is the richest person so he has no dryness of anything. The only sadness in his life is that his parents don't talk with each other. Many of times he goes sad due to the no communication between his mother and father. Many of time he has also tried for the talk but he goes in unsuccessful in that. But this is not the reason which he cares for and his nature is of that he enjoys every moment in that little age even. In school everybody knows whose son he is, so no one messes with him. His father is the trusty of that school so Vivek is the boy to whom teachers are also in little fear that if something goes wrong with Vivek due to them then they have to lose their job. The school is with of lots of facility, everything is computerized and the students have the facility of latest instruments that are available only in USA. His father ,anything that comes in any part of world if that can increase the facility of student then firstly he talks with his son about the thing and if Vivek likes that thing whatever cost that will, Maheshbhai immediately demands for that thing from that country and brings that thing to his son's school.

One day Maheshbhai, his wife and his son is on club where they are for enjoy of day. In club, Maheshbhai sits in VIP room and opens his laptop and starts his work about the planning of new venture he wants to start in Jharkhand. He is doing his work. Neha is a social worker so she is with other women of her NGO or other women who come there just to meet her and they are talking with each other about the society. They are discussing the situation of woman in world. Like Vivek there are lots of boys and girls also who are in club with their parents and their guardians.

Vivek calls all the children to him and says "All of you please come here."

The children goes there then Vivek adds "As all the man are in their group and all the woman are in their and they are discussing the business and about the society but they have forgotten that they are here to enjoy and not here for the discussion of serious issue. They are here to make us happy and play with us but they are not enjoying the moment but we can. "

One of the girl in the group says "How? "

Vivek replies "Stupid girl by playing we can enjoy and nothing else. "

All the boys and the girls get ready for play. Everyone starts playing by making their small different group. Vivek has taken One of their Five friends and has planned that each and everyone has to catch other one and whoever gets catch by the catcher, they both then have to catch the other one remains. They are playing after some time all four get catch and they all have to catch Vivek who remains alone. Vivek is running around the club and everybody else are following him, all of sudden Vivek sees "No Entry " board in front of him but continues his running. He is in "No entry " area and trying to get hide there. All the four are warning him about not to go in "No Entry" area but Vivek is not ready to listen to them. There is one guard who hears the voice of boys and runs towards the area.

The Guard says by warning "Hey boy, you come out from there, the place is not safe .That is no entry area. "

Vivek replies" You are also with these four and want to catch me, I will not come. "

The guard sees that Vivek is in that particular area where there is a big hole for some work. The guard runs towards Vivek very quickly, after seeing that the guard is running towards him to catch him , Vivek fasts his run and continues but very few second later the guard catches him.

He takes him in safe area and in anger says" Can't you see that this is a "No Entry" area and in this area no one is allowed to enter. If something would have gone wrong with you, you would have got injure then who would be there to take responsibility of that. "

Vivek replies " Why are you shouting at me ? I thought you are also running to catch me so I ran fast. "

The guard in anger "You stupid boy, I am teaching you that by this type mistake your life might have a trouble and you are arguing with me about. "

All of sudden Maheshbhai comes there and he hears the shouting words of the guard at his son Vivek.

He goes there and asks "What happened my boy? "

Vivek replies by crying "Look father, this guard is shouting at me. "

Maheshbhai gets angry and says" You rascal, have you had any idea who is he and at whom you are shouting? "

"Sir he went on "No entry "area and.. " . replies the guard and he is on way for completing his sentence about the danger of his son's life might have gone in danger and he is shouting just for nothing to teach Vivek about the instruction to follow so next time he would not do that type of silly mistake but in middle of that Maheshbhai stops him and says " What happened if my son went in "No entry" ,I have never rebuked him sharply and you are doing that. "

The guard replies "Sir listen to me. "

But Maheshbhai gets full angry " You fucker , keep quite otherwise I will slept you . Don't say any words after it. "

The guard is of low position and as he is not in position to explain anything to Maheshbhai as Maheshbhai is not ready to listen to him, by force he remains silent. In anger Maheshbhai goes to the manager of that club and asks him to fire that guard immediately otherwise he will complain to his higher authority and the manger also has to lose his job. The manager doesn't ask anything to the guard and immediately fires him out of his job without listening his side of explain. The manager has done that in force. The guard goes in changing room and wears his home going cloth and walks towards gate. The guard is the only earner of his house so remembering that he is walking towards the gate and cries. Maheshbhai stands there and is looking that guard going and everybody also.

The guard is walking and crying, his tears are at the par level. In that time the guard says to himself" if I wouldn't have stopped that boy at that time then at this time, the richest person of this country might be in tears. Might be he had lost his son but I had stopped and saved the life of that little boy and in against of that good work, I am losing my job and nobody is ready to listen to me. What kind of justice is this? "

The cultivation of in this incidence, the incidence shows the society of world is only of the richer man and there Is no place for the poor person who is honest and doing his duty for his family. Just for nothing the manager has fired him out of the job without hearing his explanation. This is what the guard is thinking at this time.

After some seconds Maheshbhai says in very happy gesture with smile "This will I do whoever messes with my son. My son is charm of me and I will do anything for him and can't see sadness on my son's face. "

Everybody near to Maheshbhai sees Maheshbhai and agrees with him. Some are agree with him by force and some are agree with him by lack of knowledge about the incidence.

In village Deven is in class three and by the time of his education of him, his report card has started to show that Deven is not interested in study. Many of times his father has punished him for not studying properly and many of times his mother has tried to teach him the importance of education but they both has failed in that try. Sometimes by the words of his mother, he has tried for the lesson to study carefully but he also has failed in that. Whenever he tries for the study by concentration, he feels that the noise of outside are calling him for the play . Many of times he has tried to rote his lesson like parrot by voicing his read in loud but the inner think of him continues and that inner voice thinks about the jungles ,river, money and many other idea by which he can get richer. In that thinking process Deven totally goes dissolve and his study always remains incomplete. Many of times he thinks that he is rich now and everybody is outside his house and asking him to help them. Some want thousands, some want lakh and all they are sharing all their problem to him and every time he listen to one's sad story about what has happened to him, he goes emotional with that person and immediately ask his secretary to give that person money as much as that person wants. Sometimes he thinks that not everybody is good and may be some persons are telling him their false story and they want just his money by fooling him but he is such a intelligent boy that he immediately catches the lie of people and call for police and ask them to punish that person who is lying to him. So he is the king of his think and his thinking has no limit. Sometime he flies with airplane and having competition with that flying machine and every time he wins in last second in very much drama manner. Some time he is swimming in sea and beating the whale. Sometime he is at the peak of the highest mountain and sometime he is at moon. Like this, his think has no limit and every time he sits for the study he dissolves himself in thinking and the time goes just like that. His father tough voice effects him nothing and sometime he is beaten up by his father for not studying but that doesn't matter to him but many of times when his mother advises him about study, he learns his lesson for sometime but his think has grown up day by day big on size so he has no control over his think so again he flies in thinking process. But that doesn't happen when for little time his father gives him the responsibility of the shop, he cares the shop very carefully and the transaction with the customer is even better than his father. Many of times he has thought about this that why the big thinking process doesn't come at the time when he sits in shop? That question often rounds in his brain but he doesn't get any answer. In opposite of that, Priya is in her very small age is very famous for her study. She is the superior of her class and is very intelligent in every matter. People praises her and often compares sister with bother but that is not any matter to Deven and he never jealousies of that because he loves her very much and she also loves him very much. The mutual understanding of their is so beautiful that they both can understand what the other one wants and what is the circumstances of the other one and according to that they react in that atmosphere. In night Priya is learning ,Deven is in his thinking process and Jhamkhudiben is cooking meal. Rajanbhai comes in and sees that all. He remains silent . After washing his hands, he sits for meal and also both the children.

They eat their food and Priya again goes for study . Deven is on his way for sleep, Rajanbhai sees that and says "Yah! go for sleep as you have studied that very much. How nice son you are of me? "

Deven remains silent .

Rajanbhai adds "You donkey, monkey. This is a limit of laziness, are you crazy? "

Deven is looking at his father's eyes that are full of frustration.

He adds" You are such a shame full boy that after hearing me, instead of studying you are looking at my eyes without any shame and fear. "

Deven says "Father what to do . My concentration never remains in study and I don't like to study and feels bore. "

Rajanbhai goes angry and says "If you concentrate then concentration will remain with you but you always think outside so how can you get concentration. "

Priya is there and listening all that . Priya in sign language signs Deven not to argue with father otherwise the anger of father may go high so he can beat you.

"Learn from your sister" Rajanbhai is completing his sentence in middle of that Deven ask to himself " What the sign language? "

" How intelligent she is? look the people are already praising Priya about her intelligence. In this little age she is famous that much and you are always in words of villagers for doing your some type of nonsense movement always. " Rajanbhai completes his sentence,

Deven replies "I don't care about the villagers what in the news of them. "

By hearing that Rajanbhai anger goes high "You stupid boy, I am teaching you and you are arguing with me instead of understanding. "

Rajan is searching his stick with which he often beats Deven. Priya knows that as her mother is out in neighbor's house and once her mother will come, she can stop her father and also knows that she will be there in very little time so for diverting her father's attention, she says" father look at my leg. "

Rajanbhai asks "What happen my baby? "

Priya replies "In afternoon, I was playing and glided so I was hurt by that stone near to me. "

In real that trauma was of two days before but that trauma has changed all the situation so Rajanbhai's all attention goes in injury of Priya.

" My little sweet baby, please take care next time . Is this pain you?" Rajan asks with lots of pamper ,

Priya replies "Yes father little with. "

After which Rajanbhai brings some medicine from one box and imposes that medicine in that trauma .Meanwhile in between that Jhamkhudi comes in side house after completing her talk with neighbor ,

Rajanbhai says "Why don't you take care Priya ? You don't let me know about her injury during play today. "

Before Jhamkhudi can say anything, Priya slowly signs of not to say anything about the truth. She is doing that just because of her brother. Jhamkhudi sees Deven is sleeping in his bed so she feels about what would have happened there and why Priya is acting all this.

Jhamkhudi immediately understands that matter and remains silent for some time and replies " Sorry but the injury is not big and I have already imposed medicine in that. "

As Jhamkhudi is there so everything in that house goes calm and after some time Priya also goes for sleep after completing her study.

One day in morning Rajanbhai has already gone to his shop after having some breakfast. Priya is preparing and dressing. It is the time of their school. Deven is not preparing for school.

Jhamkhudi sees that and asks him" What is going on? Isn't this time of your school? "

Deven replies "Yes mom but today I am not in mood of school. "

Jhamkhudi and priya is looking at him, he adds " Please mom let me not today. "

Jhamkhudi asks" Why? , Give me one proper reason that you think can impress me then I will let you do whatever you want to do? "

Deven smiles and replies "I don't have any excuses. My health is in good position. I have no injury and nothing anything else but please mom let me, please. "

His mother is looking at him and also Priya does,

Priya says " What brother! you should give some excuse for that. Tell her that this happen to you or that happen to you. It is so easy. "

Jhamkhudi is observing all the situation and she says "Yes she is right. Give that to me. "

Deven replies "No mom, I can't. I just want to tell you the truth and the truth is that today I am not in mood of school. "

Deven never says lie to anybody. He is the one, it looks like that he is made of truth and the other reason for his always saying truth is that he is the one who is never in fear of anything. Fear is the big reason why people gives excuses and excuses is the one which creates the false sentence in your mind and after which whatever you say that is the reason of your fear and the falseness. In other word when your mind develops, it means the intelligent think is coming on your way and when you are intelligent then you will handle the problem according to the situation and the situation can say you that in this situation you must have to say the wrong or lie to other person then only you will be out of that situation which you are going on. So the big reason for your lie is fear,

fear makes your mind about the situation clear that if you are going to say the truth, you will loss either that thing or that thing .That makes your mind sharper so about situation and what will come out of your mouth that will be a big sentence of falseness . That doesn't mean that intelligent always talk lie but that means that maturity and intelligence teach you that you have to open your mouth according to the situation and situation can say you that you have to say the truth to handle this situation or situation can say you that you have to say lie this time to handle this situation. Jhamkhudi has observed that Priya is intelligent so she can say lie to anybody to handle the situation if that situation demands that she can say lie that time and in other hand, Deven is fearless and Deven feels that if something goes wrong by his wordings then that will be handled by him as he is the maker of that situation then he can handle that also. Jhamkhudi realizes that the matter of Deven never has grown up so high as people know that his sentence are right and Deven knows that if he is right then he has no reason to fear of anything. Jhamkhudi is thinking all this and Deven and Priya is looking at her and waiting for her decision to come out.

Jhamkhudi says "O.k my boy you are allowed to remain in house but at one condition. "

Deven without any waste of time asks her "What I have to do? "

Jhamkhudi replies " I know you are here so you will definitely go for play but today after playing for some time, you have to study for one hour and that is not in your normal way but with concentration and in afternoon time, you have to sleep at least for one hour and in evening again after plying for some hour, you have to study with again concentration. "

Priya asks " Mother you will be on your duty after some time so how will you know about that your son will do according to your instruction. "

Deven looks at priya with different manner.

With a big smile on her face Jhamkhudi replies " Today, I am also not in mood for job so I have decided not to go for job. What you say my son ?"

Deven smiles and makes his face the word yes."

first promise me after which I will allow you. " She adds

With the word promise Deven goes upset in very next second and in very boring mood replies " O.k I promise I will do as you have told me. "

Jhamkhudi says" O.k now you are allowed . Now I am going with your sister in school to drop her and till then play with your friends and I will be here after some time so you also will have to come within two hour after playing. "

"O.k mom "replies Deven and runs away outside the house.

Priya says "I am agree with father that yours so much love to Deven has corrupted my big brother. "

Jhamkhudi with love " I know that but today whatever I have done that is for his goodness. I am sure today he will study his lesson carefully and other reason are there but leave that and ready for school , I will drop you. "

Jhamkhudi takes her daughter to school and in school she clarifies to master about the reason why her son has dropped school today and returns to home. After some time of playing, Deven returns to home and as per his promise, he is studying his books carefully with concentration more than ever.

Jhamkhudi is looking at him and says "Good. "

In noon time Rajan comes to house and sees Deven in home. They have argument about this why she has allowed him to stay in house but she with calm explain to her husband with reason and Jhamkhudi is the one with whom Rajan always after anger slows down his anger. In other word, jhamkhudi has very powerful explanation power. She replies according to the mind of person and situation of any matter. So Rajan eats his lunch and again goes to his shop. In noon time as per Deven's promise, he goes for sleep. Jhamkhudi is outside talking with her neighbor. The day is very cloudy and the atmosphere of that day is very dark. In the time of day, one can see the night darkness so everybody is little afraid about what is going to happen so that this type of atmosphere all of sudden in village. In house Deven sideways in sleep and the hurricane lamp is near to him that is because of the darkness. Jhamkhudi has put the hurricane lamp with fire on in it and in that sideways the hurricane lamp rolls round and falls in the grass of house. All of sudden, fire catches all the house, Jhamkhudi sees that and her neighbor immediately asks everyone for help. Jhamkhudi realizes that her son is in home so without any care of herself, she runs inside house where Deven is asking for help. In inside the house, almost fire has grown up so badly to whole house. In middle of house Deven stands and ask for help. The temperature of house is on high because of that fire,

Deven is shouting "help, help, mom please help me. "

His mother sees that and she starts crying. For the first time she has lost her patience and in that time her mind is asking what to do and not working properly. She only wants to save her son from that fire nothing else. In middle of Jhamkhudi and Deven, there is one big wood and that wood is firing so high. Because the house is made of wood ,bamboo, and grasses so the fire catches and rounds all over house so quickly that Deven does not get any time to run out of house. There are big wood that are roof for that house and that all are burning so fast. Jhamkhudi by her leg kicking that burning wood which is on floor but that wood is so heavy that the wood is not siding away by her force so she decides to side away that wood by her hands. she catches that wood from one side and tries to push that little so somehow she can get way to reach her son. In all this Jhamkhudi's hands gets burn but she doesn't care about this and By some efforts she makes successful herself and reaches to her son.

She takes her and tries to run away but her sari catches fire by the wave of fire so she asks her son with fear" Go my son, take that straight way and run so fast that may hurt you but by that only you can save your life . I am coming just before you so run my child run. "

Deven immediately runs fast on straight way and goes out of

house. In behind him, Jhamkhudi also runs after stifling her sari's fire but all of sudden the upper wood falls in head of her so hard that she goes unconscious and she falls in floor and the fire catches whole of her body. In outside, people are throwing water on that house but that much of water is not enough to stifle that fire. So quickly fire goes high so the smoke goes above that fire and all the people of village come to know about the fire. Far away from that Rajanbhai in shop sees that some one's house is burning so he runs immediately there but in middle of that way he sees that fire is coming from his house side so he speed up his run. He reaches his house and sees that Deven is outside the house and some of his body's part burned,

Rajanbhai comes to Deven and asks him in very hurry with fear on his face" Where is your mom? "

Deven is crying and in continue cry he replies "Mom came to me to save me and she called me for fast run so I ran so fast from inside the house after that I don't know what is going on inside, she is inside the house. "

Rajanbhai with no second think tries to go inside house but some people of village catches him immediately.

One of them says " Don't be crazy, there is no chance to go inside house. You may also go burn so stop here. We are trying so hard to stifle that fire ".

Rajanbhai shouts with cry "leave me, please leave me. My wife is inside the house, I want to save her so please leave me. "

Everybody looks at him and throwing water in that house. By the wave of fire some of the fire flies in that area and also catches fire some of that house's neighbor house but as people know that and throws water so the burn of other house doesn't injure any of the person of village. As that is the cloudy day. Everybody is praying to god to have a rain so that rain can stifle the fire but that is the only to show cloud and even not a single drop falls in earth and because of that everybody feels unfair. After half an hour people get successful to stifle that fire fully. All goes destroy, the house has nothing left in. Some of the people goes inside house and bring the burn dead body of jhamkhudi outside house. Rajan runs and reaches to her, he is crying and crying and says " Why you left me alone? why? I don't want to live without you, also want to die, please take me with you. "

All the women also start to cry, one of the woman says "she was so good. "

The other one says "God has done injustice. "

Third one says "She was so helpful. "

Fourth one says "Is this an age to die? she was so young and in that young age god has taken away her from us. "

One of the old lady says "Instead of her, god, why don't you haven't taken me with you? "

Men of the village also talking with each other,

one says "Yes, she was good woman and I wish her rest in peace. "

One of the old man says " My grandfather had once told me, God in heaven and is alone so he need good people from us and so he takes away good people so early with him. Jhamkhudi is one of the good people of his list so he takes away her at her young age. "

Everybody there agrees with that old man and like this the talk of people continues. Deven is looking at his mother's dead body which is covered by white cloth. Deven and his sister stand near to their mother's dead body and crying so much. The atmosphere of village is totally in sorrow. Everybody is trying to motivate three family members but their tears are outing from them like river. After some hour, people decide to burn Jhamkhudi's dead body as early as possible. They take away that dead body to cemetery where Rajanbhai burns her dead body according to the pure hindu religion process with so much cry and cry.

Rajanbhai is very sad. People are taking him from cemetery. He is crying so much that all his body is out of his control. One or two time he faints down on ground,

People says him " Please have a control over yourself. It is the destiny and no one can change destiny."

Rajan's house has burned fully so Deven and priya are there in neighbor's house. Everybody is saluting Jhamkhudi for her sacrifice she has done. She has saved her son's life without caring for herself and that's what people are talking about.

Rajanbhai is coming with lots of crying noise and tears he says" Why you left me alone, without you I am nothing. I had very wish full list about you that I wanted to spent time with you. I had wish to buy jewelry for you which you would have worn and on seeing on mirror, you would be so happy that you hug me. I had a wish some day in future, we would be on travel to see the great place of Gujarat. I had wish, why god this too early? am I have done anything wrong then punish me but why she? She was a pure soul who had never done anything wrong to anybody, is that was her fault? tell me god, you have to answer my question. "

Saying all this, he reaches the neighbor house where after hearing the crying voice of Rajanbhai, his children come out. They are there, Priya is also crying for her mother and Deven is very emotionally crying. The wordings of people are rounding in mind of Rajanbhai . As soon as the children come out, Rajanbhai with no time after seeing his son, immediately slaps so hard Deven that Deven falls down on ground .

People get surprise and asks " Are you crazy? what is this? why you slapped him? "

Rajanbhai in lots of anger replies" Yes I am crazy. This boy has made me crazy. If today he would not have demanded for holiday from school, she would have not put holiday from her work. This all would have not happened so at this time she would have alive. I am shame full to have this type of boy because of whom she never had a happy moment. She was not died because of fire but she was killed by him. "

Rajanbhai again goes to Deven to hit him with his leg but people catches him and stops him from doing that.

One says" That small boy, he is so small and all whatever

happened today is just an accident and all is our destiny. No one is ahead of his or her destiny. "

Deven is looking at his father and his emotion. He is very hard boy who never falls of himself believe at any point of time else than after seeing death of his mother but this time, he has much tears on his eyes because his father has put that concept in his mind that his mother was killed by him, he is responsible for all that. He runs to open ground near that house and lies down on sand. After some hour thinking there the atmosphere goes nigh with the night.The situation of Deven is of like the prisoner who feels own self culprit for his fault that is what with Deven that Deven after hearing the words of his father blames to his mirror heart as a guilty one. He is looking at the star and not saying any words but in his mind he is thinking all the scene of today and he feels that yes that was his mistake and he is responsible for his mother's death. His mind is now repeating these all things again and again and repeating all the words to himself. He throws sands here to there and he is slapping himself by remembering his father's words again and again and this is the night which is like nightmare to him which is not passing itself. Every second is like the whole time of hell to him. In house after so much of cry Priya's body loses her stamina and sleeps on her neighbor's palm after which she is taken away to bed. Rajan is there standing and thinking all the memory of his wife and his tears are continuing all the time. In sand Deven also goes sleep because of lots thinking process in his mind.

The very next day Deven in 5 am wakes up. Deven is on sand, nobody came there to take him home. After some time, all the cocks of village start their crowing. Deven comes to neighbor's house where Rajan is there and Rajan is looking at him in anger. Deven does not speak any word and runs away in side house. For the first time Deven is that much of serious. For some days all that process of crying continues. People of village make Rajan's house again, a little small than the older one by collecting funds from villagers, of woods, grasses and bamboos. All the three are now back on their house. After some days, Rajan is now a drunken person. He totally forgets all his duty towards his family and is drinking day and night. So all the responsibility of house is now on Deven. Now Deven is very serious person at that little age. He decides to leave his school and just to focus on the shop and home. In morning time after cooking and preparing his sister, he drops her at school after which he goes to shop to transact as Rajan has left the shop and has decided to drink only and nothing else. In night time Deven comes from shop and cooks food for family.

Deven always gives meal to his father and every time his father throws that meal on face of Deven and says" Don't try to feed me. I am not your father and you are not son of me. "

His son looks to him emotionally,

Rajan adds" Don't look at me. I don't want to see your face. Your eyes are dirt, your body is dirt and in reality you are made of dirt. "

Priya tries to stop him but Deven stops her.

Rajan continues" You are not a human, you are that spider

who eats his mother from inside to grow up. If I would have any idea that one day you would kill my wife then I would have killed you immediately after your birth. "

He stops for few second and sees Deven again and again adds" You are everything of hell demon and even worse than hell demon. Hell demon is nothing in front of you. "

The anger of Rajan to his son is like fire. Like fire sees nothing in front of himself and catches everything on his hand and burns them of his range and only water can stop fire so as Rajan is now like a fire and he wants to burn Deven on his anger . In this space water was Jhamkhudi only who could stop him like many of times she had done that. Deven realizes the value of his mother in life of his father. He realizes that his father was always like this time but his mother had that type of ability and intelligence that every time his father had behaved in this manner, his mother had stopped him with her love and care so love fully and that was the real importance of Jhamkhudi in that house. She was the soul of that house and Rajan feels his body without his soul. This time Priya is near to him but Rajan even don't care about her. Rajan was that much of habitual of his wife that without her, he can't imagine his life. The thirst of his life was only his wife and she was not there so he thinks the anger of Rajan to Deven is from his side is right and so correct that the meaning of life means to him was her. After all this sentences which are thrown to Deven by his father, Rajan throws some things of house also here and there. Rajan doesn't want to see Deven's face so he goes out of the house.

Priya says " Stop father , where are you going ? please don't go. "

Her father with lots of cuteness replies" I am going to hell my baby. Your mother has left me alone and she has gone In heaven and right now I am facing hell so I have to drink to face the position of this hell and have to sustain in this hell and for sustaining here I have to drink and the bottle is not here so I am going for drink. Only that bottle of drink can give me the power to sustain here otherwise the memory of your mother always reminds me of her and the emptiness I feel after her. "

Priya remembers the moment of past where every time how his father had took care of her. How he had seen her little trauma in big size ,how all the wishes of her, he had tried to full fill. Remembering all these

she again says " Please father don't go, I need you. "

Rajan replies" My sweet baby, I am always with you and you know that I am in this life just because of you otherwise I would have killed myself after your mother's death. You don't know my pain is increasing and increasing day by day that much that I can't handle my pain but I am here just because of you. Please don't stop me, let me go otherwise I won't able to handle my control. "

Looking at his son, he adds "Otherwise I will kill someone in my anger so please don't stop me. You are my child and no one else is here to me. My baby, I will come back very soon. You after eating please go for sleep and have a nice dream. In morning when you are going to open your eyes, I will be there in front of you. "

In all this Priya walks to him and holds her father's hand and after saying all these, he takes her hand and puts her hand side and goes outside the house. Priya knows that her father will not come before morning,

She stops eating and says to his brother " My hunger has died so now I don't want to eat. "

Deven in pain full voice says" You and I both know where he is going. If you don't eat because of that, he is not going to stop by your hunger and not going to stop his leg from going there so please eat. "

Priya says " I know you are not responsible for our mother's death. I know she loved me that much as to you and more to our father. She had always taught us to live with love . If she had saved you that means how much she loved you . I know her and I know the love of her to us. "

Priya is just four year old but her maturity level is beyond her age . Her thinking ability is god gifted so every time she says anything, it doesn't look like the four year old baby is saying all that but It looks like that the very mature person is saying all that . Priya in that little age has understood the reason of her mother's death and she has accepted all these very quickly in her life unlike her father.

Deven replies " Priya you don't understand it. Whatever our father is saying all, this is right. I have realized that I am responsible for death of our mother. Yes father is right if I had not wished that day for holiday, all that didn't have happen and our mother would have alive this time. "

Priya wants to explain but Deven stands up and goes to wash utensil of house. Priya realizes that If she goes to him and try to explain him then definitely he will not understand that so she decides to tell everything to her master and may be master can realize Deven that he is not responsible for all that. In mid night time everyone is sleeping so as Deven and also his sister. Suddenly something sounds to his ear. In past when his mother was alive, he used to sleep with no care but tonight so much responsibility is with him and so much tension in his mind that a little noise wakes him up in any time of his sleep. After hearing the noise, he comes out from the house and sees his father is couching on sand . He thinks that if he will go there and ask him to come inside house then his father will surely going to refuse and will make noise so everybody may go disturb and the idea to wake up his sister and ask her to make his father come inside is dropped by him because he thinks that the idea may work or may be not but the sleep of both will definitely ruin out so he brings blanket from house and covers him from that after which he again goes to sleep.

On next day in very morning time Deven wakes up and does all household work of his house then he cooks food for his family. His father is sleeping outside house so without disturbing him he cleans inside and outside house by broom.

Then he wakes up his sister and says to her" Father is sleeping outside the house in sand so go to him and ask him to come inside as he has started his sleep very late night. Ask him to come inside and sleep here. "

As per her brother's instruction Priya goes to her father and by touching him, she says" Father, come inside and sleep. "

Her father after some try of Priya wakes up and takes bottle of liquor from his pocket and drinks. All these are going on and people of village are looking at him and whispering about him.

Priya says" People are looking at you and saying bad about you. Please father whatever you want to do , do that inside the house. "

Her father looks around him and says" I don't care about anybody. "

After completing his bottle, he throws that bottle up his head and goes inside the house and falls on bed and again sleeps. Priya prepares herself ready for school after some time. Deven packs her tiffin and drops her to school after which he goes to his shop. In school Priya is walking and searching for her master, she sees him and goes to him. Her master is talking to the parents of one student and is advising what to do and what not to do to care their children.

Priya comes near to him and says" Sir I want to say something. "

Master is talking with parents but replies "Yes say what you want to say. "

Priya says "Not here sir, somewhere in one on one lonely place please. "

Master knows that she is brilliant and without any big matter she would not have told like that.

Master replies "Go there in that room. That is empty, I will be there in few minutes. "

Priya with heading her head says" O.k sir I am going there. "

After completing his talk with parents, he goes to that room where Priya is walking here to there with lots of tension on her face. She is waiting for her master to talk with her.

Master sees all that and with entering in that room asks" Priya, What happen to you? Why are you so tense today? "

Priya runs to him and goes to say word, mean while master stops her. He takes her to bench and says "Before starting, sit on bench and take relax for few second after which you are allowed to start. "

Master knows the reason what he is doing. Priya sits in bench and takes relax for few second.

Master says her" Now you can say whatever you want to say. "

Priya replies "There are lots of big problem going on in my house sir ".

Her master says "Continue. "

Priya adds "My father drinks liquor all the time and believes that his son is responsible for his wife's death so he always scolds him for that and my brother is on tension all the time. "

Master says" I know about your father and I also know about your brother's tension of responsibility of whole house and the blame of death of your mother. "

She is looking at his eyes, he adds "What type of help you want from me? "

Priya replies " My father is half without my mother and I know that even with any type of advise to him , he will not ready to understand. His solution is only time, by the pass of time only, he will understand all the thing. "

Master says" Yes that is right. Your father's mind set is very narrow from beginning and after what all happened in that day, he would have believed that Deven is responsible for that death. Almost impossible to realize him what is right and what is wrong. "

Priya says" The real problem is of Deven . After so much scold from my father, he also feels that he is responsible for my mother's death and because of this, he has totally lost his self. Before that incidence he has his own charm but after that incidence, he is totally in depression. You don't know sir, he is now totally different than before. He does not eat properly , does not care about his health ,without any reason want to work. I have seen many of times he wakes up in mid night and cry for what had happened. "

After some silent she asks "Can you help him to get out of it? "

Master says " This is a pure sign of depression as you have told me. May be, he always blames himself in his own mind and mind is that thing if you don't care mind then mind starts his game own self. Whatever you think if you blame yourself even you haven't done that, your body will start to suffer due to the pressure you have created in your mind. In all this universe we have invented all type machine just because of this mind. We are different from other animal of this planet that is all because of this mind. Everything we have done is due to this mind and everything we suffer again due to this mind. Your brother is the one boy who has taken pressure of your mother death on his self so due to that all is not right to him. "

Master goes in front of her and just for nothing starts to draw something in black board and adds "This is a good job by you that you have realized this so early and came to me for help. You don't know this type of matter is different from other matter. In this type of matter, maximum of people do not understand if we will try them to realize this all the reason. "

Priya by putting her hand in her head says" Yes sir, I have tried that with brother but he doesn't want listen to me. He doesn't want to understand my words. "

Master says" I know that this type of person understand it only by passage of time when in their memory that such type of incidence will go dim but this process may take much time. It is depend on the type of accident that was. Means if the incidence from which people are suffering is not really dark then it will go dim in short time but if that incidence is much dark, then can't say the time by which that incidence will go dim. "

Priya asks" So what's the solution ? only time? "

Master replies "The other solution. "

Priya in surprise asks "The Other solution, what do you mean by that? "

Master replies kindly " The other solution means With one

bad incidence your brother's mind always think about that for him. We have to create the other incidence of same type in which we have to teach him that he is not responsible for all that what had happened. "

Priya says" Sir I am confuse. Is this that much easy sir? "

Master replies "No, this is not an easy task. For saying it looks like easy but this can be very dangerous to the person who is doing this and also for the person for whom that person is doing that. "

Priya immediately says "I am ready for any type danger for my brother. "

Master sees love for her brother in her eyes and says" O.k, for this time now, you go to the class. I have to also go to teach students and in between this hour I will plan for what we have to do for this solution. "

Priya in very eager way " O.k sir. "

Saying this, she runs to class and master also walks to class. In class master teaches something and says his students to do work related to that and in between that, he thinks planning of what to do for Deven so that he can get recovered. In class, Priya is also thinking about this. In all this the school hour passes.

The bell of school rings. All the students are running outside school. Priya is there in class silentl. One of priya's friend sees that priya is not packing her bag,

she asks "What happen to you, don't you have intention to go home? "

Priya replies " I have some work with sir so after some time I will go to home. Don't wait for me. "

Her friend says "Reading and Reading and always reading. Don't you have any another work else than reading miss ranker? "

Priya is silent and replies nothing to her.

Her friend says " O.k ,o.k ,If you are here means some important work will be there definitely . My friend if you wish then I am available for you if you want me. "

Priya replies "Don't worry, Thank you for asking me for your support but I will handle it alone . You will go late so don't worry, I will manage. You go. "

Her friend says "As you wish. "

She goes out of the school. Priya goes to that same room of morning where master is waiting for her.

With entering in room Priya says "Sorry for the wait sir. "

Master says" It's o.k , come and sit in bench. "

Priya asks" So what's the plan? "

Master says "I have thought all hour of class . Was very confuse about what to do . Finally got this idea. "

Priya asks" Which idea sir? "

Master says" As you know Between your house and this school, there is one open ground and near to that ground one small pond is there. People says that pond is cursed and ghost are there so people generally don't go there. What you have to do is, tomorrow in school time when your brother will way of dropping you in school , when that pond will come, what you have to say to your brother is that your leg goes dirt so you want to wash your leg in pond. Surely your brother will stop you but convince him by starting the drama of crying. I know your brother, he fears of nothing so after some time he will go agree. Stop your brother near to the pond and you have to go to border of pond, act of some washing after which you will have to skid in pond and as I know your brother , he will jump also. I will be there but in hidden mode that your brother won't be able to see me and you also know that he doesn't know swimming so he won't able to save you. After all this I will handle all thing but you are so small and it is easy but not easy for you. There will be danger, It is dangerous. "

Priya replies "Two things are there. I believe you 100% that if you will care then nothing will go wrong and if anything will go wrong, you will handle and the other thing is that I can do anything for my brother. "

Master smiles and feels her love to her brother and says "I hope everything will go as per our plan. "

In all this conversation, time goes very fast so master decides that he will drop her to her home.

In mid way of her home, master says "And another thing, there is no curse or ghost in that pond. Many of times, I was in that pond's way in night time and I found nothing there. All these are rumors of people. "

Priya replies laughing "Ghost may be there or may be not but my brother's ghost is bigger than that ghost and I want to kill that ghost. "

Master also laughs at her sentence. They reach at her house. Priya till mid night is thinking about that plan and sleeps in. After some time, she hears something and she wakes up. She sees that her father is yet not at house and her brother in corner is crying.

She says to own self" Don't worry brother, this is your last night of pain and after tomorrow morning, you don't have to suffer like this. I will try full and master will get you out of this. "

Innocence is light of little children if that is out of them, the children are like the clock without cell means they will like alive but when you check that children closely, you will find that they are only of show and nothing else. If innocence is in childhood that means in future that children will remember their childhood as good one. When they will be on sad mood and will have lots of tension on them then they will remember their childhood and will say, what a innocent boy I was in my childhood! . Somebody please return my childhood, I want to live that time again and again. That is your memory of life time. Some children have bad childhood due to some bad incidence and more often due to their parents or teachers or society or any of other person who effects their childhood so badly. They forget that they are child and innocence is the charm of their and behaves in serious manner. No matter how much they get success in their future, no matter how much popular they will be , they are always going to miss their childhood . The time when nothing matters to them, the time when everyone is friend of their. The time when the demand of their are like a cute sweet laugh to everyone. The time when the mind always do what only they want, simplicity is there and everyone loves them. That is the time of enjoy when nothing comes to you and you come to nothing. That is the part when we are only the part of population not the tension. That all is part of our life and everyone loves that one. Deven is in currently that position that all innocence of him is out of him. He feels himself like the prisoner who is passing through the crime and that crime will remain always with him forever. He feels that his crime is above all universe crime and nobody can save him for that. That means that if he will alive in future just because of life that he has lived and the crime which he thinks of done by him is nothing less than the punishment of hell.

Next day early in the morning, Deven wakes up very early in the morning, starts his work of household. Listening to that Priya also wakes up and sees to him. Like early days, he has lots of tears in his eyes, tears are always in his eyes but sometime it falls down and sometime it remains in eyes of him. Priya goes near to her brother and sees him with emotional eyes.

Seeing all these, Deven asks" What happen to you? "

Priya continues to look at him without any word.

Deven gets surprise and again asks" Sister, what happen?, why you wake up so early in this morning? "

Priya sees him and replies" Nothing Brother, today my wish will come true and when the wish is going to fulfill , how can a person sleep ?, I am just thinking about that and so. "

Deven does not understand what she is saying so asks" Which wish and what are you talking about? "

Priya replies" Time will say everything to you so wait for that. "

Deven says" You know, you are answering just like mother. She was like this, she answered all but just in other way that always people realized a bit of map that will make a hint to them for their answer to search. "

Priya smiles a little and says" Like mother like daughter. After all I am her daughter and generally daughters are shadow of their father but I am the one, I believe that I am totally like mother and that's makes me feel proud always. "

Hearing all these, Deven's tears come out of his eyes, he closes his eyes and remembers the face of his mother and the fall of tears increases and increases.

Priya also cries and says" I remember my last memory with mother was of when she dropped me to school and in between that I had great fun with her as she was joking, teaching, talking with me and with the people of village and finally she dropped me to school. That was nice moment of my life and I will remember that forever as a last memory with mother. "

She stops for a while and her brother is totally on tears.

She asks" What was yours? "

Deven replies" Let it go, I don't want to talk about that. "

Priya says" Come on brother, whatever was mine, I have told you so why not you? I want to know. "

Deven replies" In that afternoon, I was not sleeping as I was not habitual of that. She came to me and told me that she knew about strange thing doing and so I had promised so I had to full fill that and I was just by force on bed. She told that whatever I was, she was proud of that . She had full trust on me. She added that I was her diamond whom she never wanted to get away from her. She told that she wanted that whatever I would do in future that must be according to my terms and condition so that she would feel happy that her son was living as per his own terms and final sentence that I had heard was that she had full trust on me that I could do anything . Might be, she had told after that also but I felt that sentences so seriously that my eyes went automatically shut down sleep. "

By hitting on his face own self, he adds" But I had broken all her believe. Just because of me, she is not with us at this time. I am not nice son. Due to me only, our father is suffering that much in this time. If I had not done that silly mistake that day, our mother would be alive at this time. "

Priya knows his condition so that she neither try to stop him from crying nor she goes for any explanation as she knows that he will not understand anything. As always he completes his work and Priya prepares herself own. Her father drinks and sleeps. Priya is ready to go for school so her brother also to drop. In walking time, Priya is thinking about the plan and thinking about her sir, is sir there will be or not? Thinking all this and trusting to her sir, she is ready for that plan but all of sudden in middle of village,

one old man comes to them and says" Hey Deven how are you? "

In village , there is no work for old man maximum time. They are there to just gossip and gossip and for that they look at one fix place where they can gossip about the village and all the condition of country.

Deven replies "Fine uncle. "

The old man looks to Priya and says" Hey you naughty girl and what about you? "

Priya is thinking about their plan so she doesn't have attention there, looking this Deven puts his hand on Priya's shoulder and says" Hey Priya, uncle is asking something, please reply. "

Priya gets her attention there and says" What uncle? What you have asked? "

The old man with smile on his face "May be something naughty intelligent think is going on in your mind as I know you. I have asked that how are you, my little baby? "

Priya also smiles and replies" Not naughty but intelligent think is going on in my mind and I am absolutely fine uncle. "

The old man sees some shine in her face and realizes that she is planning very big today. The experience of old man has taught him the understanding of realizing the shine which he has seen just now in Priya's face so he decides to remain with them to see what she is planning and how she will promulgate that.

He is eager to see that so he asks Deven " Where are you going my boy? "

Deven replies " To drop sister to school and after that I will be on my shop to handle that. "

The old man says "I have some work that side so may I also join you. "

Immediately after listening this sentence, Priya thinks about her plan so she replies "How can this be possible uncle? I know this time is of you to have cigarettes in that under the middle tree of village with your age friends and the time is of gossip of village ,what is going on? What is wrong and what is right? And all that will remain half without you so how can this be possible uncle? "

listening this, the eagerness of that old man rises on high and he is for sure that something will going to happen and that he wants to see that .

Deven with humble says "Sorry for my sister's sentence. Hey priya, may be he has some work there and that will benefit us that uncle will be with us so you can uncle, you can be with us and that is no question to ask. "

Priya goes upset with that and The old man says" Yes I have the work there so I will. "

They all start walking towards school and the lake is almost near to them where master is waiting for them to come. Priya is in confusion what to do or what not to do, so she thinks of the way of truth for solution. Deven and the old man are walking so priya also. Priya slowly throws her pencil from her bag and walks of.

Some second after She says "Brother my pencil is missing , I have put that in my pocket. "

Deven says " Did you forget that in home?"

Priya replies " No brother, I have that just before few minutes and now that is missing. "

Deven is confuse, generally Priya doesn't do that type of silly mistake, she cares her all thing.

Deven says "So what to do now, missing means missing. Take one from any of your classmate in school ,that you can. "

The old man is listening all the conversation. Priya makes a drama and says "There, I can see that pencil there, can't you? "

Deven replies "Yes I can, I am going there . You both just wait for few second , I will bring that."

Saying this, Deven walks towards pencil.

Here Priya joints her both her hands and says" I beg you uncle, I will tell you everything next time. Please for now just make a reason and go back to village. Please uncle, I beg you, this is an emergency and the need. "

The old man sees emotion and the truth in her eyes so he says" Promise me, you will tell everything to me as after all those long years gossiping in under that middle tree of village, I am habitual of all this and always eager to know anything this type of. "

Priya says" I promise. "

Deven is back there and the old man says" My boy, I remember, I have some work there in my house so I have to go back there. "

Deven replies" As you wish uncle. "

After that the old man goes back. Priya and Deven are near to lake, Priya sees her sir behind one of tree, so this is time for her to apply their plan .

She starts playing and jumping and she puts her leg on one little sheer of mud and says" Oh! No, my leg goes dirt, what to do now? "

Deven says "What is going on today ?continue to walk towards school , will handle everything in school. "

Priya says "No, I can't like this . There is a lake so I am going there to wash it. "

Deven says " O.k just go fast and wash your leg as early as possible . We are getting late for school. "

Priya replies "O.k brother. "

The lake is on little slope so she gives her bag to her brother and she very slowly tries to subside to lake. She is looking at her brother and own self slide to lake. As she is very small and doesn't know how to swim, it gets serious after she slide to lake and she slide in deeper place of that lake . She is shouting to her brother for help and her brother immediately jumps on. Deven is on lake and he catches his sister's hand but there is inner wave which is dragging them inside lake so both of them are shouting for help. Listening to this Sir runs so fast towards lake and jumps in lake. The master is not that much old and so also have the experience of handling that type of inner wave and the power also. He swims and gets catch both of them with his ability, he brings both of them out of that lake. He puts down both of them and presses both stomachs together. As Deven is little long than priya so he first gets his health back. He sees that Priya is unconscious and master is pressing her stomach and trying hard to get all that lake's water get out of her . He is seeing all this and praying to god for his sister. The master processes that in right way and Priya also gets conscious. The plan of Master was not that much serious but in his plan, he had not thought about the inner wave of lake and that inner wave of that lake had made that real and Priya was on really in danger.

Deven says" Thank god, she is o.k. Thank you sir for saving our life. "

Master says" That's o.k ."

Priya goes better also so she says "All is my fault, I have made that silly mistake and due to that, me and my brother's life was on danger . I am so silly that I hadn't realized that, If something would have gone wrong to my brother, I would not have ever forgiven myself for this."

Deven replies "You have done nothing wrong. Don't feel bad, we are o.k and nothing had happened to us so forget about this and let it go. More than myself your life was on danger and I am happy that you are o.k . "

Priya says " But brother........ "

Deven in mid of her sentence says" You are my dear one and for you, I can do anything. This was my care , love and everything to you so don't bother about this. If something would have happened to me for that you would be not responsible ever. "

Master sees in his eyes and says" That is what we want to say to you. "

Deven asks" What, what you want to say? I am not understanding anything. "

Master replies" This all was our plan to make you realize that in time of your mother's death, it was her care , love for you because of which, without caring for herself, she had saved you and sacrificed her life just for you as like you have done just now for your sister. This was the planning of us but her life was really in danger. After hearing the help word from your sister, you thought nothing about your life and immediately jumped on this lake even though you don't know swimming so as your mother had done at that time. She also loved that much you, in here your life was on danger and so as your sister's life was and you had gone for your sister so as your life was on danger at that time and your mother's also but she decided to save you . You don't know how to swim but just because of your sister, you jump in this lake to save your sister's life. No matter how much that could be dangerous to you. You know Deven if there is someone who is in danger, some people help them and some people let that go but if at that place, any one's dear one is on danger, no matter how danger there is, anyone won't think about that danger, they just want their dear one to save for which they take their life at risk. Just as you have done, your mother had also done. My boy realize it. "

Priya says" Remember you have told today in morning that our mother wanted that she wish that you will live your life at your terms and condition so please forgive yourself for what happened that day. You are not responsible and you never be. Our mother was great and she wanted that we will live our life greatly. "

Deven is listening to them and thinking about all that. He cries and hugs his sister emotionally. They all get up from there and walk towards school. In their walk, there is lots of silence. One can hear pin drop sound there. They all reach school where Deven drops his sister and walks away from there without any word to anyone.

After her brother's walk, Priya asks" Sir ,Deven is walking without any word to us. I am In confusion that whether he had understood or not, what we wanted him to realize. Shall we have to do this type of plan again where I will have to put my life ,yours and brother's life in danger again? I am very much in fear after what had happened to us just now. "

Master smiles and replies "Don't worry, we don't have to. He is going in silence means he is thinking all about our sentence and in this type of process it will generally take time even after our experiment. All is depend on the person's mind with whom we are experimenting. Now his mind will say to him and he will realize what we wanted to say to him so live him alone. I know he will understand all this. "

Priya also smiles and says " I have full trust on you . It is my pleasure to have such type of sir like you who teaches not only the lesson of book but also the lesson of life. Thank you sir. "

Master says" Without a nice student, a teacher is always remains half so I am happy that I have student like you. "

They both go to class after this conversation. In other side, after some time, Deven reaches to his shop. He is on silence and just doing all transaction with very few words that are needed. In Evening time Deven is cooking food and Priya is near to him. Priya sees his face and starts talking about the funny incidence of her class . Priya is telling all incidence and Deven laughs at her sentence . All the corner of house are on happy moment. After her mother's death, Priya has seen that laugh for the first time. She has realized that their plan has worked and Deven has started forgiving himself. Seeing all this priya feels very happy and tears automatically comes out of her eyes. All of sudden her father comes in from outside, he has drunk and is smelling liquor. In this light moment,

Rajan sees laugh at his son's face so he goes in irritating mood and says" My wife's killer is laughing and this is ridiculous that he is laughing at her house. This has happened to nobody. I am helpless otherwise I would have killed him but this is my destination that he is brother of my sweet baby so I am helpless. "

After some silence, he shouts" God, are you listening, I am helpless. "

Priya and Deven are listening him and see anger on his eyes,

Priya says" Father come here to me , I am your daughter . Please sit with me at least for some time . I remember that how much you have loved before , I was your heart so what happen now? "

Rajan replies" You were not my heart, you are my heart . You want me to sit with you so I am coming. "

Rajan goes to his daughter and sits close to her. His smell of liquor is unbearable but Priya adjusts herself somehow.

She says" I am your daughter so for me only can't you forget all that please. "

Her father replies" My baby, how can I forget all that and how can I forgive this bloody killer. Don't again ask me to do this . I can't and I will never. "

Deven says" O.k don't forgive me and I know it is hard for you to forgive me but just for Priya, can't you just talk to her and love her? "

His father again shouts" You bloody killer, don't talk to me. I love my daughter and just for her I am here. "

Rajan remains silent for few second and adds "My baby, I will, from tomorrow, I will. just for you I will but don't aspect from me to have any mercy to this killer. "

Deven is happy by his reply so he asks his sister to say yes in sign language.

Priya says" Not from tomorrow, I want you to do this from just now. Promise me , you will be at house at time in evening always. I won't stop you from drinking but you have to promise me that you will be at house on evening time and as you wish after that . Just love me nobody else, is it o.k for you? "

Her father replies " My sweet baby, I am always o.k for you. "

Heading his head up down, he kisses his daughter on forehead. Deven is satisfy so as Priya. After so long time, In that house everything has happened good. After some time Deven completes cooking and Priya serves to her father as both of them know if Deven would have served then their father definitely wouldn't have eaten so. After so long time Rajan is eating evening's meal at his own house. Deven is standing some far and looking at them. His father is feeding his sister and his sister is feeding his father. He is happy that at least that had happened. After they both finish their meal ,Rajan goes to bed and Priya starts reading her book. Deven goes there and eat meal after which he washes utensils and cleans house. After which priya also goes to sleep so as Deven.

In other side, Ahmedabad city next day , it is a birthday of Vivek . His father wakes up early in the morning . He has all the readiness for his son but he waits for his son to wake up.

His mother is also there and she is cooking some special item for her son . She wants to feed her son made of her own hand so she is in kitchen. The whole house is in shine, everything is according to Vivek's choice .At nearly 9 am Vivek wakes up in his bedroom, in outside there are all people waiting for him. Vivek washes his face and brushes his teeth after which as soon as he opens the door, the musician starts the music of happy birthday to you. Whole house is surrounding with the rhythm of happy birthday to you. Before this time Vivek has got his birthday celebration but this is not expected of him to have such warm birthday wish in very early in the morning. There are more than 25 musicians with their instruments and all they are playing for him .His father comes to him and hugs him with sentence of happy birthday to him. His father brings him in big drawing room where one specially made king size throne is put before.

Vivek says" Wow what is it? Is it for me? "

His father replies " This is throne which is specially made just for you in England. I have ordered them to make so that my son can feel like king. Please son sit on this throne and just make it feel that someone very special person is sitting on it and make it proud for that. "

Vivek sits on that throne. Music is on sound in that round continues in, sounding very pure to all. Vivek's mother comes there with carrot halwa in her hand. She goes near to him and feed him that halwa with her hand .

Vivek says" Wow mom, you know this day is very special to me because I love this carrot halwa and this is the only day when you made it by your own hand and feed me always. I can tell you if there are lots of people's halwa are there and I have to choose which one is yours, surely I can find yours cooking. I simply love this, thank you mom for this. "

He looks to his father and with smile on his face says" And thank you father for all this, thank you for make me feel like a king. I love both of you very much. "

His father comes to him and gives him a little suitcase.

Vivek with surprise asks" What is this father? "

Maheshbhai replies" In this suitcase money is in it and as today is your birthday so I want you to give bonus to all these musicians and servant .They have done their job and I am very happy with their work so this is extra payment to them for their work and you will give this to all. "

Listening to this, all the servants and musicians get happy.

Maheshbhai adds" All of you have to come, one by one, my son will give you bonus for your work. "

Vivek gives money to them and all the persons are giving blessing for this. After which Vivek prepares for school, Vivek is in table for meal ,

Maheshbhai says him"In night, there is a big party in Rajkash club so you can call any of your friends and teachers for that. "

Vivek asks" Why on club father? we always celebrate my birthday in our house, don't we? "

His father replies" Yeah, I know that but for this time, I have made some special arrangements there for your surprise. That's why son. "

Vivek replies" Oh! I see. I will father, I will call all my classmates and all my teachers for my birthday party. "

After having meal Vivek goes to school where he asks every classmate and every teacher to attend his birthday party for sure. In evening time everybody is on club. All the climate of club is like heaven. The decoration is made by designer from Scotland, all the arrangement are of high class. Maheshbhai has spent millions of rupees in that party. All are waiting for cut of cake by Vivek. Vivek is on way to cut the cake, all of sudden the noise of private chopper comes to everybody. Everybody is on surprise specially Vivek after seeing his favorite film star Jha rukh khan in his party. Jha rukh khan is the top most celebrity of bollywood. His demand in all over world is over high. He is the top most celebrity and charges millions of rupees for his film and also just for his attendance at any party. He is the person who is not affordable even by top most richman.

Jha rukh khan comes to Vivek and says" My dear one, happy birthday to you. "

Vivek says" Oh my god, is this really you? you don't know, you are my favorite star and love you so much. "

Vivek looks to his father and asks" Is this the surprise you want to give me? I just love this surprise, this is the best surprise to me till now. I love you father. "

His father replies "Me too , And yah this is your surprise".

Jha rukh khan says" Your father is dear friend of me and he said that I am your favorite star and wants me to attend this birthday celebration. I just took time from my busy schedule out and I am here for you to wish you happy birthday to you. "

Vivek looking at the real star and his favorite film star says "So humble you are that you took time for me, you make my this birthday above shine of Dog star on sky. "

After that Vivek cuts the cake and the whole sky surrounds with fire crackers writing on the sky" HAPPY BIRTHDAY VIVEK". Everybody on club is happy, the party overs in 12:30 am nearly after which the family of Patel are going to their home. The driver is driving and all the family members are there on car. As road is empty so driver speed up the car, all of sudden driver lost his control over car due to the other car's strike in cross road . The car gets back by that strike. Accident happens there but everybody in that car are o.k and just get some scratch three of them . Only the driver gets little injure by that accident. All the family members get out of that car so as the driver,

Vivek says" It is horrible. "

Neha says" Can't believe this, I am in fear. "

The driver says "Madam it is horrible but the good thing is that nobody gets badly injure, thanks to god. "

Maheshbhai searches In his pocket and touches that thing and says" I know why we are safe but I want to thank this for god so day after tomorrow we are going to have visit to any of lord Shiva temple. Which temple I don't know for now but will tell you in morning after some search. "

They call for ambulance and get discharge early in the morning. In morning, it is 11 am and in his house,

Maheshbhai says "I have decided that for this time, tomorrow we are going to The Balaram temple near mount abu. That is famous lord Shiva temple. "

Neha heads her head as she has no other option and says to Vivek " Get ready for Balaram temple this time my boy. "

Saying this she goes to bedroom.

Vivek says "O.k father. "

Vivek goes to phone, calls one of his friends of school and asks all about the temple and he gets all idea. He goes to his father in one special room where not everyone is allowed. Vivek sees that his father is putting something on one of the box there,

he asks" What is that father? "

His father sees him and says" Oh! You are here. Come and have a sit with me. "

That room is very special with computerized lock on door which can only be opened by one password that is known only to Maheshbhai. The whole room is full of furniture and there are lots of little boxes.

Vivek asks again "Father you don't reply to me, what was that which you have just put on that little box? "

His father takes that box out from that furniture and replies "It is "THE COIN. "

Vivek gets surprise by his answer and says" What "THE COIN"? "

His father replies " Yes "THE COIN". "

Vivek asks" Why is this so important and why you have put this on this special room? "

His father is looking at him and Vivek adds" Is it of billions of dollar? "

His father replies " It is priceless. "

Maheshbhai takes that coin out of box in his hand. That coin is shining, that is like star and that has the quality that one can automatically attracted to that without any gravity.

Vivek says "Wow! What a beautiful peace this is! Can I touch it and have this one in my hand? "

Maheshbhai replies "Why not son, you can. After all in future you will be the owner of this and you have to take care of this. "

Vivek asks" You just told me that it is priceless, can I know why? "

Maheshbhai replies" In late seventeen century when almost in whole India there was British and they were in india to rule the whole country. They were there to rule India by the excuse of business. At that time, our forefather was a servant of king of that time. By the time went passed, The general british came here and he was here for business so he was the guest of king. So that was the duty of our forefather to served him and gave him the best of service . He was here for almost 3 years and at that time between the general got very impress with our forefather's duty. Our forefather had done his duty with that most honesty that once he had saved the general's life without caring of his own life. At the end of his time when he was going to England , he had given this coin to our forefather for his duty and for saving life of the general and had told that this coin was made in England long ago but this was made with that type of material that it would never get rust. It was the coin of luck with whom this coin would remain, that person would be lucky . The luck would come to that person automatically. The general had put that for so long and he felt that this coin was deserved by our forefather for his work. From that time, this coin is with our family. "

Vivek asks "You mean to say that in present whatever is with us that is just because of this coin? "

Maheshbhai replies" Yes, the coin has made its luck to us. Due to this only, we are here at this position. It has helped many of time to me to get out of any problem there to me so I believe in this and this is reality. "

Vivek takes that coin in his hand and says" Wow! What a feeling just by touching it! Now I am also agree with you father. "

Maheshbhai says" Yes I know , just touching it in your hand gives that type of energy that nobody will ever want to let this away from himself. It is powerful. It is the sense of inner joy. "

Vivek says" Yes father, I am feeling very nice. "

Maheshbhai says" Do you know in last night why we were so lucky that nobody of us got injured badly ? It is just because of it. In that accident if somebody else would be there so they might had caused danger to their life. After that accident I had immediately touched this coin to ensure that whether this was with me or not and I found that. We are so lucky that I had put this coin with me last night . I generally take this out with me if there would be some special work and last night was your birthday and your birthday is always special to me and see what this coin had done, the big word magic , saved our life and we are o.k here. "

Vivek says" Oh! Father thank you so much for that, I am proud of you always. "

Vivek after some second says "Today I have found this room open may be you forgot to close it but I found always password lock . My dear father ,may I know the password? "

Maheshbhai says" Anything for you my dear one but make a promise not to say it to anybody not even with your dear one."

Vivek immediately says "I promise father. "

Maheshbhai says " It is V…I…V…M…A…H FOREVER. "

After thinking for some second Vivek says " It means Vivek Mahesh forever. "

Maheshbhai says "Yes it is ,I love you more than anyone. "

Vivek hugs him and says " I love you too father. "

After few seconds,

Maheshbhai Asks" By the way, why you came here following me? "

Vivek replies" Yah! I have forgotten that listening to this coin. I am here to say something father. "

Maheshbhai says " Yah! Tell me. "

Vivek replies "In my class, one friend of me had once visited his village travelling by local train of Gujarat and he had praised that travel so much that the journey of local train was mind blowing of him. He had described that journey to all of us and at that time I had wished once to travel by local train and we are going to THE BALARAM temple. I have just called one of my school friend and got all the idea that we can travel that temple by local train so I am here. "

Maheshbhai says" Do you know we have never travelled by local train even not by train so how can and how can we go temple by local train my boy? "

Vivek replies" From Ahmedabad we have a train at approx 7 am and that will leave us to Palanpur and after which we can travel through bus and that will just take approx 45 minute to reach in our destination by bus. We can either take taxi or any other vehicle. We will be there in time father. "

Maheshbhai says " That's good but how can we son? Are you sure you want to go by local train then by bus? that may cause our health because generally local train are dirty and lots of people will be there so due to that much crowd, we might face suffocation problem son. "

Vivek replies " I know father , my friend had already told that to me but that is a life and I want to enjoy that . I want to enjoy the moment in local train only once and after this I will never ask you to do this type of any travel by local train . I am wishing it and I know you. "

Maheshbhai says" Now you are emotionally blackmailing me but everything for you my boy. If you have this wish, I am here to you to fulfill your wish, my charm. "

Vivek says" Thank you father, I know you are going to be convinced. Now I am going to mother to have permission for this as she will also with us and I know she will also agree for this. "

Maheshbhai by his wife's discussion only goes silent and just by sign heads his head. Vivek goes to his mother and also convinces her for local train travel of tomorrow. In late night Vivek is sleeping in his room so as other,

Vivek wakes up and says" from that time when I have touched that coin , in my mind, the coin has made a way and I again want to touch that coin. That coin has given so much pleasure to me that I can't say about that even. "

He gets up from his bed and goes to that room, there is a password if anyone try more than 2 password in one time, the alarm will automatically ring out and Vivek knows what is the password. He thinks about that password, he is in confusion whether he should open it or not. He is thinking whether he is doing right or wrong but he goes with his wishes. By that password, the door of that room opens and Vivek feels the love of his father to him.

Vivek with smile and by giving flying kiss says "I love you father. "

In room there are lots of small boxes but he has seen his father putting that coin in one box and which was special box so Vivek goes to that box and opens that and takes that coin in his hand. By the feeling of that touch, he says "Father has told that this coin he carries with him on special occasion and I think visiting temple is always special to him so for this time I will carry this coin with me. "

Thinking this, he takes that coin with him and shut the door of room again and goes to sleep in his bedroom.

THE COIN, In mid of fifteen century there was a rule of queen Elizabethy in The great Britain. Once she was visiting her garden alone in night time. She saw that one shining thing fall down in her garden from sky. She went near to that and saw that one small stone was there. She tried to take that but that was so hot that no one could touch that even . She brought one metal utensil and by one iron stick she put that stone in that utensil. She went to her bedroom where she put that stone in one utensil which was full of water. She saw that in which utensil she had brought that stone also went fire and a big hole was there in that. To be cold that stone had taken over more than one weak and during that time, she had used many utensil with water because that stone made any utensil a big hole .After that stone got chilled that much that she could touch that. One day after some days over week, she saw that the stone got chilled that she could touch that . She took that stone in her hand and that stone gave her that much of pleasure because of which she forgot all her tension. After which she put that stone always with her. By the time she felt that after that stone entrance in her life, her time had become great to her. She had solved every problem of her .She felt about the luck of that stone. One day she thought to make that stone turn in to one coin so that she could easily took that with her so with that idea she ordered one of her trustable one to made that in to the coin and in that stone put the symbol of star one side and in other side put the symbol of T. As per her guidance, the stone was turned in to coin by her trustable person. She was very happy and her era was called the golden age of any time . She had solved problem of her and globalised her idea so that everyone could live there life happily . Her era was of 1555 to 1602. In 1598 once she was visiting her land and she saw a poor worker with lots of tension , she found that the problem of him was above any problem so realized that there were lots of problem everywhere and that was for always . She thought keeping that coin would make only her lucky but passing it through different hands could solve problem of more so she gave that coin to that worker and asked him to put that coin with him and after his condition would get very good, he had to gave that to the other needy one. After some years of that, Elizabethy's era got over and after that, that coin went to different hands of different people. That coin reached to the general and the general gave that to The patel but he forgot to told him the sentence of queen which was repeated by every owner of that coin so from that time the coin is with the Patel family.

In morning Deven wakes up at 5 am and in city Vivek also wakes up at 5 am. It is co-incidence that both have opened their eyes in same time. In village Deven starts his household work and in city Vivek goes to his parents room to call them about the good morning wake up so that they can prepare them self to visit temple .In village Deven is holding his grass and arranging them and in city, Vivek is in his parents room. There are two bed in that room, one is for his mother and the other one is for his father as they don't speak to each other so they don't sleep in one bed, Vivek goes in middle of both bed and says "Good morning. "

There comes no reply of it so again says but this time in louder voice " Good morning. "

This time his mother wakes up and replies " Good morning my son, is there any problem so that you are here? "she says it looking at her watch.

Vivek replies "Mom you forget that we had planning to visit temple and I have told you the whole idea so I am here. "

Listening to this his father wakes up and says "Please son, can we go by our own car at late at noon? "

Vivek replies with naughty irritation eye "No father this is not possible. I have made complete planning and you are messing my planning? "

His mother replies "Yes, can we please? my sleep is incomplete and give me some more hour to complete it, please son. As we all know we are not habitual of rising at this time like some other people. "

Vivek says" No, you both have to wake up. "

His mother asks him" How you have opened your eyes so early as you always wake up after us and that is too with lots of try? "

Vivek replies "That's the magic. "

His mother asks "What kind of magic? "

he says " Nothing. "

He replies to own self inside " The magic of the coin , due to which just thinking about it and holding in hand and seeing that again and again so never went really for sleep, Wow! ."

His mother says "Please son. "

Listening to this, her husband stands up in floor to pass comment at her " I am going to ready , anything for you my boy. Some people don't know that early rising is good for health and having always lazy means rising late from bed, what you say my boy? "

Listening to this, his wife gets irritate of that but she doesn't reply anything and goes to washroom.

Vivek says "Yes father you are right and I salute you for being the controller of this house. "

His father says" Yes I am and always be and now please don't waste the time, go to your room and be ready for the visit by your wish of The local train. "

Vivek says "Yes , I am going. "

Answering it, he goes to his room and Maheshbhai also goes in other washroom to do his gas work. It is a 6 and 15 minute am Deven has done his cleaning work and also has cut the bundle of wood by axe. Deven is cooking meal for his members. Now it is 6 and 20 minutes, in city,

Vivek is ready with little small bag and asking to his parents" Mom, dad, how much time? We will get late and we will miss the train so do it as early as possible. "

Running towards Vivek, Maheshbhai replies "I am ready son with you to fly. "

Vivek calls his mother" Mom, what are you doing, we are getting late, please mom. "

Almost after 15 minute, she comes outside and replies "Now I am ready, we will get late. Just do it fast and let's go. "

Listening to this Vivek replies " MOM!!!! "

They come outside the house. They all gets in ,The driver of the car starts the car,

Vivek says "Uncle please fly the car, this is a morning time and this is so early to have a traffic so fly the car and lift us to railway station as early as possible.

The driver replies "As you order little master. "

The driver now in talks with air and the roads are empty so they reach in railway station just in 35 minutes . It generally takes 50 minutes to 1 hour. Now it is a 7 and 10 minute,

Vivek says " The train was of 7 am and we are late . My whole idea goes to mess , this is upsetting me. "

His father replies" Don't worry my son, I am going to ask the inquiry man about it and if we had missed the train, we will go by car and next time in other temple will be on local train if that will be on local area , don't worry. "

He goes to the inquiry man and asks" Hello, what about the local train of 7 am? "

The man replies "Sorry for the inconvenience but the train is half hour late so you have to wait."

Maheshbhai says " Thank god, please give me three ticket of Palanpur. "

The inquiry man replies " Just for people like you, just because for whom these trains gets late to take you in them. "

Maheshbhai knows the real reason but he is not in mood to argue with and he knows that the inquiry man don't know with whom he is talking so he comes to his son and wife and says" We have missed that. "

Vivek says " Oh! No , shit!, this just because of your mom. "

Nehaben sees a smile in her husband's face as her husband wants him to have that blame on her.

She goes to Vivek and replies slowly in his ear "I will do a magic and the plan will not have to cancel. "

Vivek asks" What magic? "

She replies " Just Wait for few second silently. "

Maheshbhai comes to him and showing the ticket "Just joking, this is a ticket and the train is half an hour late so let's go to the platform and will have to wait there. "

Vivek says" Oh! Really, mom , you are so great and father you are also. Let's go to platform. "

They go to platform. There are lots of crowd and due to that Neha and Maheahbhai gets irritate and frustrate but Vivek is enjoying the crowd so much. He walks here to there in platform to enjoy . Sometimes he plays with his age buddy and sometimes he talks with old age grandfather. He is enjoying that so much. The train gets late and late due to technical mistake and at 8 and 20 minute the train arrives at platform and people are running to have a seat in that . People are running towards it without the wait of train to stop and some people catches also that in running. Few second after train stops and everybody is busy in to get their seat so there is so much buffet and in between that Maheshbhai and family is also trying to get seat. The first problem is that of how to get in to that train because of lots of people are there in door and trying to get in. Maheshbhai also decides to have some anger in that so they can get in . So he pushes some people here and some people there and takes his family inside. In inside he runs so fast and gets one seat of three people.

After sitting in seat Maheshbhai says in anger" What these people think about themselves and about me? Even I can get local train seat and that is even in my first trip in local train. Yes I can. "

Vivek laughs and Nehaben smiles at him and Vivek says "Wow! Father this much anger, I have never seen this type of frustration on you, this is brilliant. "

Maheshbhai replies with smile "Thank you son but this is for first time and I am enjoying it and also enjoying by remembering that buffet to me in that door. "

Vivek says" I know father that you are going to enjoy this trip like me and what about mom you? "

Nehaben is not feeling good but just to make happy him, she heads her head up and down. There is crowd and people of tea seller and the singer little girl who are bagging from people to have money for them also. Maheshbhai gives them 100 rupees each and all the people are surprised by that because gencrally they get 5 rupees and even less. They have wore high class cloth and spending money lot more but in local train and seeing all this, people of that cabin gets surprise. There is bridge in after some time that bridge is of just track . There is two side and that two side are joint bye just track ,in which if we see down from train door, it's look like the train is flying on air and nothing is down under it. That type of track bridge are generally attach to village and after bridge there are jungle or city way so that type bridge is the only place where the children of village can stand under it. Vivek also sees that type of bridge from window and that scene is really enjoyed by him. He sees from window that under bridge there are some children and they are asking for money and people are throwing 1, 2 and 5 rupees coins to them and the children are fighting to have that one . Some children get that and some children don't. Vivek also wants to do that so he asks to his father to give him some coins and his father without any care gives him total of five coins . Vivek goes to the door, people are asking him to remain in inside but he wants to do that so he doesn't care about the words of people. In first of bridge of that type, he throws one coin and under that bridge and one child gets that and looking that Vivek gets very happy. In village Deven is ready to drop his sister to school so as Priya is ready to go school. This time they are talking to each other in way, joking, laughing and everything. He drops her to school and is going to his shop.

One of Deven's friend comes to him and asks to him" I have some work with you, shall you come with me please? "

Deven replies "I am going to shop so I have no time. "

The friend replies to his reply "I know that but I need you and enjoyable also so please. "

Deven thinks about that and yet not has said yes to him.

The friend says" You are my friend, people dies for friendship and this is a small work and you don't just want to come with me, how selfish you are !"

Deven replies "O.k let's go, I will open shop after some time. "

His friend takes him to the bridge track of that village where there are some children and above all, one 14 year old boy Jignesh who is longer and stronger than any of them is also there. What Jignesh is doing is that he is longer of all and stronger also so when any person of train throws a coin there, he takes that away by his ability of long leg and strongness. All the children are there from morning but nobody has got any money just because of Jignesh.

Deven asks" Why you bring me here? You know that I don't like all this so why? "

The friend replies" I know my friend that but for this time I need you. This boy called Jignesh is doing what is taking all the money so once when I have tried to have one coin so he threw me out and also got that coin. I was so angry at that time that I made there one bet that we the children would get at least one coin before 10 am and that is for sure. He also agreed to that condition and replied to me that if any children would get any coin then he would give up all his collection to me and I was helpless here . I couldn't do anything and he was getting all the coin till now and still he is getting that so I was searching for you and found you near school so bring you here. What you have to do is to get just one coin and all will be mine. "

Deven says" Before a bet, you must have to see your abilities and in which condition you see you and myself to have any one coin. Didn't you think before that bet? "

The friend rubs his head and replies" I know this but at that time I was so angry and in anger I saw nothing and just made that bet. "

Deven says" When you brought me here, you told that this would be enjoyable but it doesn't look like enjoyable and Loosing by you may not cause anything so lose my friend lose. Why are you risking your life in this ? look at his arms, they are so strong. "

The friend replies "That is true and after that bet I had realized that what I had made but after that bet I have no other option but to do otherwise. "

He stops there and doesn't complete his words so Deven asks "Otherwise what? "

The friend replies "Otherwise I have to give him 500 rupees for loosing. "

Deven says " What? Are you crazy? Don't you have any sense what are you talking about? "

The friend replies " I was out of control at that time so I made that silly mistake. You know that 500 means even that I won't get in that 500 in my three month. "

Deven says "Stupid, that won't you get even after 1 year . You are getting one rupee day by day and there are only 365 days in year and cut the holiday when you won't get your one rupee so how will you? "

The friend says in tension" Oh! Really, my friend please take me out of this. I know you are fearless so you can do this. "

Deven replies" I am fearless but I am not senseless. "

The friend goes upset and Deven looks to him and Deven adds" Now don't think much about this. I will make some idea to have at least one coin just for your win. "

The friend replies "Thank you so much, I know are going to help so you are here. Now this is 9 and 40 minute so you have not much time to think about. You have to do this as early as possible. "

Deven stands there and says " Go and have a try . I will try after all the analysis of his position and the area of this place."

The friend replies " O.k but please try your best to help me."

Deven makes a fake smile in his face as he knows that it's going to be tough. Deven sees Jignesh and area for 10 minute and Deven is looking at every position of that area and how Jignesh is getting all the coin. Deven calls his friend and make one idea to get that coin. Vivek in train is enjoying lot more, he is throwing his rupees to children under bridge. Every time a bridge comes, he throws one coin and have his own enjoyment. The train is on way, it is near to the village of Deven where everybody is looking for train to come. Deven stands there very silently and observing the thing. The train is on that bridge and all children are asking to have coin . Vivek has already thrown all his left pocket coins so he is in hurry and he forgets all the other thing out of his mind, he searches in other pocket and finds one, He immediately throws that under bridge. Deven runs after seeing this, it is like the coin is on air and Deven is running towards it to get that. Deven dives all of sudden in running moment and gets that coin.

Without seeing the coin which he holds and he holds that one tight in his hand.

Jignesh in anger comes near to him and asks" Hey boy, give that coin to me, Otherwise what will be a mess to your face and that you are going to responsible for that by your own self. I will get that somehow but just think about yourself, brother. "

Everybody there are seeing that and in sign saying not to give that one to Jignesh. Deven is in confusion what to do and what not to do. All of sudden he starts running, Jignesh also runs behind him so as the friend of Deven, in running Jignesh says " Hey you stupid, stop, stop there otherwise I will kill you. "

Deven makes his running fast , Jignesh is running behind him and in anger again says" You donkey , now I will kill you. "

The running is going on , Jignesh gets tire of that so he again says " Hey my sweet friend , shall we have some compromise please . I will give you half of my money but for that you have to stop , please stop. "

Saying all this Jignesh stops own self. His stamina has given answer to him.

The friend of Deven reaches to Jignesh and asks" What happen? I know you can't catch him so forget all about that and give all that money of your pocket to me. "

Jignesh swells and taking deep air again and again and replies" If I refuse to give that to you, what will you do? You caterpillar. "

The friend replies" Nothing but remember that your ego is never going to forget this. The ego will say to you that even after losing to that caterpillar, you are happy. Why? whenever you will in future going to use any money at that time you will remember me always for not giving this money of your lose and that is enough to me and I am happy just by this win and If you don't want to give that to me, that's o.k to me but that won't ever be o.k to you and for your memory. "

His answer has deep impact on him in just few seconds. Jignesh thinks about that and he finds that answer very correct. Jignesh is stronger but everyone has his breaking point. Emotions of sense like that answer are always a worlds most dangerous of weapon to anybody. One can't rule the world by type of power but with this type of sense one can and the people will also like that. Jignesh takes all his money out of his pocket and gives all that to that boy.

Jignesh is arrogant so he says" You are the winner of today but that doesn't mean that you will be forever. I will wait for my turn. "

The friend replies " O.k I will also wait . Every dog has his day so as you will have . Like I am a caterpillar ,you are a dog who is waiting for his day so wait for that and all the best to you. "

The friend walks away from there and jignesh also does that. Deven is still running, he reaches his shop where without looking at that coin, he puts that coin in his pocket after which he opens his shop and gets busy in transaction of shop. After some hour when shop is free of transactions, he thinks about that coin that he has caught and run but didn't see how much that was of. He takes his hand to his pocket to see the value of that. He takes that out in his hand and what he sees is that coin is shining . He feels the enjoyment of putting that coin in his hand . That coin is THE COIN of Patel's family . In morning when Vivek was packing his bag, he felt that he would be alone without that coin and his father also brought that coin with him whenever he felt that that was special occasion so thinking this he put that coin in his right pocket. When he was in train, he forgot all and lost totally in his enjoyment so in his enjoyment , he threw that coin for the children under bridge and by co-incident Deven dived for that and got that. THE COIN is in his hand and thinking about that how much It will be of. He backs that coin, he sees one side star and other side English alphabet T. He gets surprise by that coin . that coin giving him inner joy and he is feeling that. Firstly he thinks that may be that coin is of gold but after some observation, he feels that it is not. By some time he realizes that this coin neither of gold nor of copper and even not of any mental that is in his known.

He thinks" This not of gold , not of copper , not of aluminum and not of any mental of I know so what is this in real of and what is the value of it ? Really in confusion , may be this is fake coin and I am just wasting my time in it. "

He throws that coin to hump of sand near his shop and says" Nobody will take you my fake coin , even instead of that may be I will hear some abuse word due to you so good bye. "

That coin goes inside sand , Deven also again gets busy in his customer. In night time, he is in his home and cooks meal for his family. Everybody eats dinner and after some time goes to sleep. Deven also after finishing his work goes to bed. He is closing his eyes but sleep is not near to him. He feels some blankness in himself . He is thinking the reason behind this. Whenever he closes his eyes, he sees that coin only in front of him . It is like a big star in sky and that star is so near to him that he even can touch that and due to that, whole universe is shining. He gets up from his bed, he feels that THE COIN is the reason that is why In shop he was feeling that something was missing by him after every transaction to customer.

He calls his sister" Sister I am going to shop , I have some work there so I am going to complete that. "

Priya gets shock and replies" Brother in this time ? you know how much there will be darkness outside our area and you are going to shop, Have you gone made? "

Deven says" May be there is darkness outside area but I am shining. "

Priya says "What are you talking about, I am not understanding that really. "

Deven says" Just don't try to understand it . It is matter of star. What you have to do is just to take care of yourself and father, I will be soon here. "

Priya doesn't understand that but she thinks the importance of that work so replies" O.k , but just do back at home as early as possible and you also take care of yourself. "

Deven starts his walk towards his shop and takes torch with

him to see. There is really very much darkness . Deven is not afraid of darkness . He never but the way is of about 30 minutes long and in that long walk he is only thinking about that coin . Just feeling that pleasure of that coin and between sometime he also calls himself dull for his decision to throw that coin in sand. He reaches his shop and starts his search in that sand hump. He searches for THE COIN but not finding that one. He tries very hard but no result comes in his favor, after sometime he loses his patience and shouts" I am leaving it. "

By saying this word , he hits sand hard to upper side and one sound come to his ear tinnnnnnnnnnnnnng....... What he sees is that The coin is in air and shining. The shine flashes in his eyes, by smile he catches that coin again and again shouts "I got it. "

He puts that coin in his pocket and is coming to his home. It is nearly 12:30 am. He is on his way , all of sudden , he sees that one person is walking towards bramble. Deven follows that person. The person is with suitcase in his hand, Deven tries to see his face but he is unable to do that. The person scoops land there in bramble and puts that suitcase in that sheer, fills up that sheer by sand and makes one mark of cross stick and stands. Deven is near him behind some bramble so the person doesn't see him. The person goes from there .Deven is in confusion whether to see in that suitcase or not, in last he decides to see . He goes there and unearths that place, he pulls that suitcase and opens that one. What he sees, lots of money in that suitcase. That much of money he has never seen even in his dream so he goes dazzle totally. He has no control over him . He is thinking what to do or not to do. He shuts suitcase and make that place as it was before. He goes to his home where he puts that money in one secure place. He behaves very normal for some days as there is nothing has happened to him. This is the best thing which every person tries to do if something like this happens to anyone. The person behaves in normal manner if not then that person will be on trouble. This is a common sense which is also used by Deven. After someday when Deven is on school dropping his sister, he sees his master in tension.

He asks his sister to go to her class after which he goes to master and asks" Good morning sir , today why are you on so much tension? "

The master replies "Good morning son, Nothing has happened. I am all right totally. "

Deven says" One day my mother had told me that if any person says to you that he is totally all right and his face says something else means he is lying and there must be a problem and I can feel that she was right because your tension is on your face and I can read that sir. "

The master says" Yes you are right but this problem is out of reach of any of us so there is no benefit of telling that to you. "

Deven says" May be sir but I want to know that. "

The master says" O.k my son, I am going to tell that because after few week everyone will know that so why not you first."

Deven sees to him and feels that his problem is really big so the problem fighter master for the first time saying like his.

Master adds "Everyone in this village knows that this school is in land which was gifted by the father of our landlord and this school was made by him so the property is on lease. The landlord has sent me notice of over of the lease after one month. What I have to do is to pay him 10 lakh rupees to him to get this property just in name of school so children of this village can learn. "

Deven replies "If it was a gift and was made of for children to study, how can he do like this? "

"That's true but you know the landlord. He is greedy and can do anything . He just thinks of himself and his benefits and nothing else in front of his benefits. " Replies the master, Deven after thinking for sometime says" Master I can help you. "

The master says" Do you know what are you saying? It is 10 lakh rupees not 10 rupees so you can help me. You don't know even how many zeroes there are in lakhs so please boy go to your shop and just leave this problem to time . We can't do anything , this is impossible for us. "

Deven says "Sir I have 8 lakh rupees. "

The master gets surprised by this , he sits on table and drinks water . Walks for few second and says" I can't believe this, how? "

Deven replies "One night I had some work in shop so I came there in night time and in time of returning what I had seen, one person with suitcase and in bramble, he was hiding that so I went there and found that suitcase . I brought that in home, after some days I found lonely in home so I count that and that was 8 lakh rupees . I had almost spent 3 hour to count that and that was my longest three hour of my life till now. "

The master asks" Who was that person? "

Deven replies "Don't know and really don't want to know but one thing I can say is this money is not of hard work earn otherwise that person would not have hidden that in bramble. In true earning you don't need to hide your money like this. The school is in trouble so I want to give that to you. "

The master asks" Before answering this to me what was in your mind because generally giving this much amount to anybody that doesn't happen often? "

Deven replies "Nothing sir, when I heard your problem I immediately decided to give that money to you. One think I have learnt is money is made to solve people's problem and not to increase that but today everybody is creating problem just because of money. "

The master says" Yah! That's true but how many people in real understand this. "

Deven says " You are the person who has served this village without any greed to yourself. You are the person who had help my mother in her life. I remember many of times my mother praised for you, she was the one who had always appreciated you for your work. You had taught me without any fees and teaching my sister also without fees. I remember when we were on trouble, you had helped my father to open that shop which is I am using so there is no doubt for one second before offering this money to you but the only problem is I have only 8 lakh rupees and you need 10 lakh rupees so 2 lakh rupees still short to you. "

The master says" Don't worry about that . I can adjust that. I have some contact who can give that to me and some is with me. 2 lakh rupees is affordable to me. Thank god now the children of this village don't have to stop their studies. "

Deven says "I have put that money in one bag and had already burnt that suitcase of its original so I request you to come to my house in night time after 8 pm so there I can give that to you. "

The master says "O.k son. "

In night time the master comes to Deven's house and takes that money with him. Some days after, it is in the news of villagers that master has given money to that landlord and that is of 10 lakh rupees. Everybody in village is talking about that and the landlord is also in surprise to have that.

After some days, In shop Deven is there and doing his work.

One of the distributer of wheat comes to him and says " I am here to sell some quality wheat to you so please call your boss. I want to talk to him. "

Deven is too small to believe that he is the handler of that shop.

Deven replies kindley" What can I help you sir? "

The distributer says "Oh! Boy not with you but want to talk with your boss, where is he ? please call him. "

Deven replies "Sir I am the boss, I am the handler. This shop belongs to me so I am saying to you, say what you want to say? "

The distributer gets surprised by his answer.

After few second distributer says" Sir I have a big deal to you. I know this is small shop but I am in this village because I have visited this whole area and have analyzed this area and seen your shop and this shop is the only shop covering this big area so I am here to make one deal of wheat in big quantity to you. "

Deven replies " Sir I am a small shopkeeper and have not that much of money to buy that so how can I sir? "

The distributer replies " Don't worry about that sir. I am here for your solution . I will give you this wheat in credit. What you have to do is nothing but just to sell it and earn money and after some time you will be able to pay to me and will have your benefit money also so it is a deal of profit to me and to you also . You will get benefit out of it and that is for sure . We will help to make godown so that you can put these wheat with you and that all will be in credit . When you will get benefit in future and me too, it is the best part of our deal and pleasure of me to have customer with this age. "

Deven says" That's sounds very good offer to me. "

The distributer says" Yes sir ,this is a best offer and if you catch it, you will make it. "

Deven says" Sir that's really good idea and I am accepting this. May I know how much this will cost? "

The distributer replies" The cost of wheat is around four lakh and ninety thousand and the godown construction cost will be around ten to fifteen thousand approx so the total is around five lakh to five lakh five thousand. "

Deven says "That's really a big amount. "

The distributer " I know sir but believe me after selling this you can make benefit around fifty to sixty thousand and after paying me the expenses of godown construction, the big benefit will be with you. "

Deven says" I can't believe this . Is this dream that you are here and giving me this deal. "

The distributer replies" Not at all but this deal is like a dream SIR. "

Deven says " The deal is done and please don't call me sir, I am a small shopkeeper that's it. "

The distributer replies " I am habitual of this word . You are my customer and if I will give you respect then only the customer will feel good towards me and this is my policy so I don't look how old the customer is or how much his business is, the only word that comes out of my mouth is SIR. "

The distributer helps him to make a godown in his own expenses and Deven helps him for it by supporting him for it. Deven is so happy about this and in night, he tells all this to his sister and at the time when his father is also available there. His father doesn't care and totally ignores him and his sister congrats him for this. After completion of construction of godown and deal , In the next 26 days the price of wheat rises 40% above the market price due to the loss of a big consignment by the mistake of govt. and that loss of that deal and the scarcity makes the price of wheat above the all. People are coming to Deven's shop and even big seller are there to have some big deal with him that is why the income of Deven is above ever. He has his profit just in month. The family condition of his family is now goes sufficient . He buys some clothes to his sister and father. Deven realizes the luck of the coin, firstly the suitcase with money and now the big deal of wheat. He has seen that his income has increased and that he has found whenever the coin is with him, something very good always happens to him. He also takes care that very much of that coin. The coin has given him the luck so the confidence of him is upside than ever.

One day Deven buys shoe, shoe polisher with brush and clothes to his sister and some clothes to his father, he says" From tomorrow you will wear this and will go to school wearing this. "

Priya replies " No brother , I won't . I like to wear sandal and in other side, shoes I don't like so keep that side to me ,I won't. "

Deven says " O.k as you want. "

Saying this he puts all that item one side,

He says " You don't want shoes and these other things but take these clothes and the other one is of father. You have to do one thing that you have to convince any how our father to take these clothes of him."

She says " I will try but not surely can say that he will accept this."

Devens says " I know you can."

Now He is the busy boy of village . He has no time for anything. His work has increased so as the responsibility. He is doing and caring. They don't have money problem at all. Deven is totally in understand the magic of the coin and he is aware of that. The coin has started his work that is to start serving the owner to have luck always .Deven goes very protective about the coin and the fear of losing that comes to his mind so he thinks about how to keep safe that with him and whether anyone will see this then definitely will try to steal from him so he has to do something to protect that coin. One day in noon time, he closes his shop and goes to one of the oldest tree of that village where nobody generally goes so he chooses to hide that coin under that tree so that no one can get that .

Deven's father is care free of all this money transaction but one day when he is drinking liquor in the place of liquor seller, one of the drunken man asks to him" Are you the father of Deven? "

Rajanbhai doesn't reply to him but the drunken man again says "I know you are the father of The progressing Deven. He is the boy who is progressing in this little time and this is in this little age. "

The other man says" Yes he is. The man who is a proud father of his little small son and all in the village are talking, how he has earned lots of money and respect in very short time . The boy who has maintain his family in their poor time and comes up with the boost in life. That's why he is now so famous. "

Another man says "Dirt, dirt father. This is the man who has left his family in middle storm and due to that his son has taken all the responsibility of everything in his small shoulder and has done very good in all his liabilities. "

The other drunken man says" Are you not ashamed of yourself that your son feeds you and he is the sole earner in your family. You are fully dependent on him . In this little age of him, you have to feed him instead of that he is feeding you, that's the shame of you. "

The other man says "Yah! That's true, you are the father who is big fuck and everybody knows that. "

The first drunken man says again" I know that he is the father so I have asked him about this. Hey man, your son is earning much so go and take some money from him and make some party to us. "

He makes his voice loud and stands up and adds " The dependent father of a little son. "

Rajanbhai is hurt by all those sentences. His ego goes hurt and for that he makes his another glass of drink and drinks that without water or any mix.

Rajanbhai says" Will you all of please keep quiet . I will

show you who is dependent of whom. I will show you who is the sole earner of my family and who has the big responsibility. "

After some silence, he heads his face up side the sky and adds" Deven , you stupid boy , I am coming to you to teach you the lesson of your life. "

He walks towards his shop. In mid way with continue walk he says" From childhood this boy has just distraught me and nothing else, I am coming. "

Rajanbhai reaches shop and by seeing him there, Deven gets shocked,

Deven's father says in frustration" What you want from me, tell me what you want from me? "

Deven gets shocked by this and he replies "What should I want from you? "

His father says "Just because of you, I am insulted in whole village . You always wanted to do that and now you are successful in that. "

Deven says" What are you talking about, I am totally clueless."

His father says "Don't be over smart with me, I am your father, you are not. "

Deven says "Thank god, at least you have realized that I am your son. "

His father says " But I am ashamed that you are my son. "

Deven says "I am totally confused what you want from me, say it clearly? "

His father says "People are saying that you are feeding me and I am useless. "

He says politely " Why you care about those people ? When we were in trouble at that time, these saying people had not done anything to us, just good people had helped us. After the death of mother, you are totally upset and had left everything so I have taken this shop as a responsibility and if today I am successful in this shop that's just because of my mother's bless and due to this shop, now we are in good position. We can afford things of our choice so you have to happy due to it. "

His father says "Don't you talk about my wife, you have killed her and now you are dancing on my head. "

Rajanbhai goes inside shop and slaps Deven . He pushes Deven outside shop and looks in whole shop and takes one stick from a corner. He comes outside and beats him continuously . Deven is helpless, he is just weeping by that hurt and crying and shouting,

Deven says" Don't do this father , I have done all for our family and nothing else. "

There are nobody near to shop in that time to stop him for this . Rajanbhai beats him for almost 15 minute continuously. He hits him so hard that his son is bleeding but he doesn't care about that and continues. Some people comes there by hearing the crying voice and stops Rajan . Deven is hit so hard that he is even unable to stand up, he is injured so badly.

One of the people says "What are you doing, have you gone mad? "

The other says "Nobody beats any child like this, are you crazy?"

Rajanbhai replies in anger "Yes I am mad and crazy . This shop belongs to me . I am the owner of this and I will take care of this so take this boy away from me. "

After some silence, Rajan adds" Take this boy but not to hospital because I am not going to pay for that and as you are taking him there so you have to pay for that. "

One of the man replies "Don't you care about the bill, I will pay, you wolf. "

Everybody knows that there is no benefit of saying any word to him due to his drunken position and his mind. People takes Deven first to hospital where doctor treats him and makes some stitches. In shop Rajan starts his second innings with drunken behavior. Deven is taken to home after some hour in hospital. His neighbor comes to him, she has always supported this family . Deven is on hurt with lots of pain. His neighbor helps him and salves him. In evening time when Priya comes to home, she gets surprise by seeing her brother on bed with stitches,

She runs to him and says" What happened brother, how? "

Deven is not in position even to reply , he is unable. He has totally no power to do that, just tears are coming out of his eyes. Priya's neighbor comes to Priya and says the whole incident what had happened and why? After listening that Priya also cries. That is the limit of Rajanbhai, if any one hates anyone and that continues for long time then one day will be definitely the day when his or her frustration will come out to the one whom he or she hates. Just that happens to Rajanbhai as angry frustrated man and Deven as victim . Rajanbhai has anger to his son, he sees his son everyday and his son tries to talk to him and he does not so the continue process of all this has made his mind very much the hater to his son . So when somebody tells him the success of his son and his weakness to him and the dependents of him to his son , that is not bearable to him so in all of these, he does not think about what he is doing , he has beaten him so hard with all his frustration, Deven is badly injured by that. So the frustration of Rajan has come out and after some hour at shop in evening Rajanbhai feels bad about what he has done but the sorrow of death of his wife is still with him so in one side of his mind, he is thinking about to say sorry to his son and on the other side his ego does not allow him to do that as Deven is his son and is little one in age so the love is in heart inside and he puts that just in his heart just because of his ego and the one reason of his wife's death. In late night Rajanbhai comes to his house, he sees that Deven is on bed sleeping and Priya is studying. Rajanbhai is not drunk for the first time after so long days in the night time, he comes near to Priya and asks" Hey! My baby, do you have eaten your meal or not? "

Priya does not look at him and is angry with him for what he has done.

He says " All happens and I was drunk and is realizing that I should not have done that but was angry with him so did that but I am sorry for that. "

Priya says " You have to sorry not to me but to him. "

He tries very hard to convince her but she refuses to agree with him. Just to make her happy, he goes near to Deven who is sleeping and tries to touch him but all of sudden his ego does not allow him to do that, the ego says " I am his father and he is my son ,I am his elder so why I have to sorry to him."

He sides away from and that all is seen by Priya and asks "What happen? Why you stop? "

He replies " I am his father , I am not wrong but he is. Why I have to sorry to him? "

Priya asks gently "Being the elder really mean that elder can't make mistake and if elders make mistakes, do they have right to not to be sorry to their younger? I don't think so. This is not the definition of elder and should not be. "

Understanding her word clearly but he replies "I don't know what you mean for, really what you really mean is going upside my mind so leave me alone. " Saying this he goes to drink.

Priya says "Maximum people have this problem that even though they understand that what the life want to teach them, they refuses to learn that. "

The pain of Deven remains with him almost for 20 days and the pain of his father's attack on him, how much that will survive in his mind that is depend on the capacity of him. For this 20 days, he remains in house with no position to stand up. All his father has done to him is mess of him. In these days his neighbor has really helped him so much with real duty of her neighborhood. During these days some time the pain of Deven is on unbearable mode but with the support of his sister and the love of her, he manages to get out of that. When Deven recovers well after those days health wise, He is very much hurt by that attack of his father, his emotions makes him tear boy. He thinks much about that attack . He goes to sit under a tree which is almost in jungle and that tree is of neem. He goes there and sits. He sees the leaf and without thinking, he takes some leaf of neem and eats , that eating behavior of him is not normal for him. Everything he knows about that leaf is it tastes bitter and healthy for body so he wants his memory to be healthy so he can forget that attack. He cries, the tears are on his chick for continue ,

he shouts so much loud " Why…..? "

Saying why and why? He eats almost continuous for half an hour of neem leaf with tears on his eyes . He puts the leaf forcefully to his mouth and forcefully bites them . Remembering his father that day hit, he shouts again and again and forcefully bites the neem leaf . All of sudden he jumps to sand and lies there . The tears of him are continue ,he doesn't know what he is doing but just to reduce that memory of that day, he is eating leaf , shouting ,lying on sands . When he goes tier by that, the body stamina of him answers to him by which he goes sleep there almost for two hours. In his dream, he sees that his father is running behind him and even though he runs fast, after some time he is trapped and after which his father ties him on tree and hits him with hunter and nobody is there to help him and he wakes up. Tension is limitless to what to do and what not to do. He remembers his mother memory to him, that memory gives him the power to some move on. He remembers his mother's lesson to him and every good moment with his mother. Generally it sounds rubbish that when you are in problem just give time alone to yourself, make some space to you, have some think of you and the memories will cut your problem and if not definitely will give some courage to you to fight with your problem and if that doesn't enough then go face your time and the time will change for you. That's what which happens to Deven . Thinking for some time and making his mind doing rubbish thing and the memory of his mother has helped him to have some step to come out from. If you are emotionally hurt by someone unknown then that will cause you for some time and if you are emotionally hurt by someone known then that will hurt you for longer time than your think . That's what has happened to him. He is hurt not only physically but also more mentally and the pain of body reduces in 20 days but the pain of emotion full mental condition to him will survive in him for longer time than the imagination. Deven goes to home and thinks about what is his position and in real what he should do. For some days, he only travels in village from morning to evening just to time pass. He has no idea what he is doing, the whole time of him just goes in travel here to there. Priya is also in confusion what should she advice to him, she is between her father and her brother as she loves both of them equally. One day when Deven is doing his routine work that is nothing but just to travel here to there and he is near to The master's house, Master sees him and calls him" Hey

Deven , come here. "

Deven really don't want to talk to anybody so he makes an excuse and replies "Master I am busy in thinking so please not now. "

The master says "Oh! Really then may I join you in your thinking? "

Deven replies " What? I really don't know what should I reply to this and really don't care about this. "

The master says" Even I also don't know why I have asked this to you? May be this because just to answer your rubbish answer and just to confuse you. "

Deven says " I am sorry for this . I am totally not in mood to talk with anybody so just to avoid you but now I am realizing that I am wrong. "

The master says "I know your position and from which situation you are going on . If you want, you can start your education again and I will totally support you not only financially but also emotionally. This is not force but this is a advice to you and this is your decision. I have always respected one's individual decision so all depends on you really. Just don't think that I am your master and so just to respect me, you will say yes without any agree of you. "

Deven says "Thank you sir for asking . In real I have also think about to restart my education again but the reality is this that whenever I am in home and eats meal ,my father just doesn't like me and he even doesn't like that I am eating meal and wearing his earns money . He doesn't want to speak to me but he tells Priya that somebody is care free that eats meal and have no shame of his sin. Every time he speaks up his sentence, I feel very low on myself. I feel that my father hats me and he even doesn't want to see me and that time I forcefully eat my meal just to make my sister happy but how long this should go. The irritation of my father to me is going really high to me and it's really frustrating to me so much but what should I do I really don't know. "

The master says "That's very tough, I will pray that nobody will face ever like this because the way you are living is really hard. "

Deven sees up side and says "May be. "

The master asks " Don't care about your father if he doesn't care about you, that's the only way you can come out from this and just join your education again . It sounds rubbish but this is real practical way of living anybody's life . If somebody really don't care about you and if you have tried already hard to convince him or her but the behavior of him or her doesn't change to you then just don't care about him or her because life is yours and in life there are lots of people who loves you and you can just live your whole life just with them who loves you so why to waste your life and time in that person who hates you. Just think about your sister and the other people who loves you and from this time just don't care about your father. "

Deven replies "How can you say this sir? as much as I respect you that much I respect my father and I love my father lot so it is impossible sir . Just because he doesn't love me so I also doing same like him , this can't be happened and just don't expect from me . Just tell me why you are giving such advice to me? " answers in little no expression and no clue, The answer of Deven to his master is unexpected but the master doesn't feel bad about the answer because he knows that Deven's position is worst and in worst time one can give worst answer and worst answer is the worst thing of that time.

The master says " O.k my son as you wish but in real, Sometimes being rude is good . Just think my word if you don't then you will be always in confusion and your world will remain so much small that you will narrow down your world. You are always going to be a frustrated boy and may be man. The life is always about move on just like time. Time doesn't thinks of you and it just itself go on in roll. Just think that time falls in attach with somebody or care about somebody and after some years that thing or person finishes so the time will think that just because my attachment one is not with me so why not to stop everything and just cancel this world by stopping. Just like that the life of person is so what will happen do you realize just like that everyone is attach to some people only and the other people are attach to other so the world is running otherwise life would have been stopped so early . In your life you are trying hard but your father is not convince with you . He even doesn't want to talk to you. He doesn't care about you and you think that just by stopping yourself, everything will be all right and after sometime in future you will think definitely that, that was your time and you have done nothing in that time just because of a person who has never cared about you . You have missed your life and in that time you may have enjoyed your life with someone who really loves you. "

Deven says "Really such a long lecture, don't want to feel you bad but I understand it very less so what's the catch? "

The master smiles and replies "The catch is life is all about move on, it is not about to stop but about to move on. "

Deven says "Sir please sir, I can't sir. "

The master says " O.K as you wish but don't forget to think. "

Deven walks away by saying "Good bye. "

The master doesn't force him because he knows that his work is over. Maximum people in this world don't understand the lesson just in first time if the lesson is by words and if your words has power then definitely he or she will think about that really after some time and if your words are powerful then he or she will understand, realize and implement that and that is for sure but for that one has to be patience and have to give time to other person for that. That's what has happened with Deven also as he is one of the person like other so master leaves him alone to think about that and to make his own decision. Deven comes from there and the words of master is rounding around him. After some hours of thinking Deven realizes that his father doesn't care about him really and if remains with that so will always suffer like this so this is the time for him to move on in life by which he can make a way to his life. Everybody in this world wants their own image and reputation and for that one has to step his own mind to go on for that and for that they have to sacrifice some love and have to be so courageous. The life in every second teaches us something and if not that means that we are probably not seeing the sign of life what the life wants to pretend us. Sometimes by some incidence and sometimes by people and sometimes by nature and even sometimes by the active or inactive else than human. In every time we want help, somehow life definitely teaches us to move on or what should be your next step in this process or gives us help. Same has happened to Deven and this time it is The master who has given him the idea of move on . Deven thinks about this and this is really so hard to the boy like Deven of that age to have that decision but after thinking so much he makes his decision, he thinks " If i will remain in this house, I may have love of my sister and that is for sure but my father will sure going to torture me. My mom , I had loved her very much and she had too and when she was alive, I had realized that my father used to scold me but the love of him towards his son was shown by indirect . Sometimes he had hug me and for some time he had tried to taught me by soft voice and affection which was inside. My father was real for me in that time but after the death of my mom, my father has totally ignored me. His love for me is may be inside his heart little with but he has forced that loved to never be come out and slowly slowly has killed that love for me . My father's love was over to me and that is because I know my mom was the only one whom he has loved so much . I remember one night when my mother was outside my village with my neighbor because she had some work and she needed my mother's help in that so my mother was outside village in some other village and in that night I was with him. He did not sleep that night and had walked and sit for whole night and in next day when she came, he took her inside and hug her and had some conversation of emotion. At that time I did not understand what was that and why he had done that but today I have understood it and that was nothing but the love. I don't know whether my father will ever forgive me or not but if I will be here in this house not only I will be irritated but also he will be irritated so why not to move from this house. "

He says all this to himself and all the night he thinks about this that whether he is right or not? What should he do and if really want to go outside house so where and why? what will going to happen to him and that are the obvious question that may arise to every individual . Before every major step in our life we think about the questions what ,why and the word that is included is really want to do this or not ? Sometimes we back our step and sometimes we go ahead and this is why the life always circulates. This is life and this is you and you have to take decision own self. In all this, he forgets the matter of coin , he has put that coin away from him and that's the reason all wrong goes to him of money matters because once you are in habitual of luck then that will allow you to do everything right and away of that thing and in little time all will go wrong in no time.

In next morning Deven is packing his bag and Priya wakes up and asks "What are you doing brother? "

Deven replies "I am going from here. "

Priya says "What!! what are you saying? "

Deven remains silent so priya adds " Why? "

Deven replies "You know that why? because I can't handle

this anymore my sis, how should I ?, here my mind is blocked and really has no idea what to do so I am going. "

Priya asks "But where? "

Deven says "In master's house. "

Their father just near to them listening to them and getting angry but Deven has decided,

Deven says "Not any planning but don't know but if I will get some success in life then I will call you. You will come to me, won't you? "

His father is seeing him with angry eyes but this time Deven totally ignores him. It looks like that deven's thinking and master's advice has really worked for him,

Priya thinks for some time and replies "No, I won't come leaving father alone . I love so much you but just that much I also love my father and this is not possible for me to do this so my answer is clear to you , I won't and never. "

Deven says "That's o.k, I can understand this but I will call you to come and that is for sure and not only for one time but more than limit and I respect your decision but in case you change your mind, I will always welcome you. "

Deven is crying so as Priya . Priya doesn't try to stop him because of the condition and she knows that it is right to him to be stayed in Master's house so that in life he can do something of his own choice . He hugs her and cries, his father is seeing all this but he doesn't try to stop him, Deven walks out of house saying his sister " We will be in touch but this house is not for me so I am not saying you good bye but bye to this house. "

Deven is out side door so he calls his sister to come there, Priya runs there, in slow voice he says "Just take care of you and our father. Just make sure that he won't drink much than limit and make sure that you are always going to be with him. "

He kisses her in her forehead and says "Good bye and miss you. "

Priya says "Me too and love you. "

He reaches to master's house in early morning and knocks the door. Master opens the door and after seeing his packed bag, he immediately understands all the situation so he says "You are welcome my boy. I know that you have that capacity to take such a brave decision in life and I know it is not easy to take but you have and that's the reason why I have always respected you. "

So you are welcome that is the words of master which has risen up the confidence of Deven. In master's house, there are two daughters and his wife was died so early after giving birth to her younger daughter. One daughter is of 13 years and the other one is of 10 years.

Master says "This is my elder daughter Sejal and this one who is sleeping is younger daughter Hiral.

Master turns his head towards his daughters and says " You both listen to me , from now this is your younger brother

Deven. "

Sejal says "I know father and I know all the situation so don't worry about him, I will totally take care of him. "

She looks at Deven and says "Hey! Deven how are you ?

Deven replies " Good ."

She adds " You know, your mother was best friend of me and she never took care of me like any other relation but she did that in very friendly manner so one day we decided to be the friend to each other and from that day, we had never care about the age and always used to be the friend to each other so my brother don't you ever dare to hesitate with my family otherwise I will punish you so danger. "

She laughs and her father also laughs,

Hiral wakes up and says "Who the witch is laughing so early in the morning, don't you know how to laugh, I will teach you."

Saying this she also laughs so the Deven feels the friendly way of them. The family members are friendly in certain way and they know how they should behave to avoid the ignorance in life. Deven next day again joins the school to have the study back in his life. He goes to school to have that much so now the attention of him in class is more than before . He tries to study more carefully than ever and there are his classmate and they have lots of questions to him to ask. Deven doesn't have any answer to the questions like why his father had hit him and why he has left the shop after that much success. In mid of the class, in the time of recess , he talks to his sister and saying the words of missing her. As he has no answer to his friends questions so the classmates start to tease him for that.

Some says "I know why he is here again because his father has beaten him so hard and that much so that all the ghost of shop are gone up outside by that hurt. "

The other one says "Look who is here, he used to be the brave one but this time his father don't respect him so why should us, how he can pretend to have respect from us? "

In all these, all the students laugh at him and he goes silent. This is the some days of his restart in class.

One day his master calls him and says "Listen my boy, the more you bear, the more you will be tortured so just tell them the truth and after the truth who will be with you, they are your friends and who are not, they are not understanding you. This way you can find the good one and the pressure of your silent will also will go. The truth is the one way you can really make silent to all of them and I know that you are the boy who never speaks lie and never gets in fear and that I have always seen in you so be the Real Deven and real Deven speaks truth and not the boy who remains silent. "

In real Deven has started to fear but the quality of his truthness is still with him . Fear has come to him by way of The coin, when he has got the coin and with that he has got that success in little time so he has himself created the fear of getting lost that coin and the success will go out from him. Nobody in that village knows about the luck factor of The coin so nobody also knows the way of success of him. In all the matter of his father and the tension of all that, he has forgotten the matter of coin.

Next day in class when his classmate tries to tease him for the matter so he goes in front of class and says "Listen to me guys. Yes this is true my father has beaten me up and by that I have been in bad almost for 20 days. The reason, my father has beaten up me is simple that he did not want me to be the earner of the house. May be his ego but that's the reason and that's the reason why I have left the shop and house also because my father does not want that so and lastly I want to say that, that was the hardest days of me so the Master has solved my problem and he has suggested me to join my class again. I found that suggestion suitable so I choose to be here. So my friends if you have any further quarries about me so you can come to me and ask and finally that's all from me. "

Some boys find that dare and some not but after that some students start to clap on so the whole class claps and makes feel him the proud for that. And after that the classmates don't tease him and all of them are now friend of him. Deven a boy who has never demanded high in his life but the circulation around him has always demanded high from him. It is all like some type of circulation of life which is going to him and that is the big thing of life.

In house, the conversation between Hiral and Deven is different from other.

Whenever Hiral sees Deven , she says "So bro?"

Deven completes the line every time by saying" I am fine. "

sometime he says " Getting bore. "

sometime says " really enjoying. "

The conversations between them are cute but unlike any other. Their conversations are always different. The love between them is the sweetest one in their family. Hiral never talks in straight way to him like if she wants to say "you are very intelligent." Then she will say "you are an idiot." Always in the opposite words, everything she says always to Deven in opposite words and Deven also understands that so he also talks with her in same way. That is the way they talk and the manner of their talking is liked by the other members also so sometime they all talk in same manner.

In night time all are eating, Deven says "This is very bad food, I am sure if hiral would have cooked then definitely it would be so fantastic that I might haven't eaten ever. "

Sejal says " I hate you for my criticism. "

Master says "I am surely not agree with you. "

Finding all of them in opposite of her,

Hiral replies "So if all these would have happened then I would have been very happy and always like to love you for sure. "

Deven says "Someone is very calm and I can't find any smoke out here. "

Hiral goes miff and they all get their laugh at same time.

That's all going on in his life . After the leave of his father's house, he is very to find such a cool family who not only loves him but also teaches and in every difficulty helps him for all this. Deven meets his sister Priya in school and finds out all the about the care of her and also about the making the situation so nice to her so that she can also love that to make her life without any tension. The basic idea of his living in the house of master is clear than ever and for that he is making lots care to that so he can find a way to live and also to handle the situation. In his life, master has taught him the all how to handle the situation so proper and the important angle of life so that he can live better. The mid way of the life of him is going around to take all the past of him but difficulty with him is that every time he learns a lesson about life and the other situation comes in front of him and every time he thinks that why all these are just happening to him and all the problems are coming in his way just to stop him and to make him the weakest person of life. He is a child with not much patience but little with of his age patience but every time he tries to be the calm boy and takes the situation to handle, it as he can but like in account you can't leave the old error transaction behind you and the old error transaction always comes with you in your next page and the old error transactions always effects your all the transactions of future. You can't make your a/c perfect without the remedies of old errors. Deven is in the positions of like a/c as he is not making his old transactions of life to remedy so the situations always carry forwards him to the next page of life so the problem of old pages always tries to overcome to him in such a manner that the problem are meant to be the just for him and without problem he is nothing so after all this, he convinces himself that life is difficult for him and in every phase of way, there will be some problem to him and that is for sure so he has made himself so much tough so that he can fight the life and try to come out of that. The problem may take time to be solved out but he has convinced himself that even though the problem may not be solved but the situation will favor him to come over out of that. The boy who is living in the house of master and that is all by love of them but the people are the person whose words of mouth are coming on the way of Deven and Rajanbhai.

The words to Deven are "How can be a boy so irresponsible in his life that his house is here and his sister and father are here and in all this situation, how can a boy leave his father's house and can live in other's house and he is happy in all this."

The other sentence " Deven is not good boy. He doesn't care about his family. The boy should not leave his house like this. This is so embracing and no one would like to happen like him. "

On the other side same words but from different angle to Rajanbhai "You are such a dull father. No father would like to do such as you have done and this is the reason why everyone in this village sees you with the dummy eyes. The father you are who is just made of your own self, your son is missing his house and you are not caring all this. "

Thus the words are according to the person . Deven controls himself to react to it because he knows the situation and the condition why he has left his father's house so he doesn't react but on the other side, this time again his father is on hype. Maturity is the thing which is not depend on your age, it depends on your thinking ability. That's what has happened, Rajanbhai is a very narrow mind person, so the mind of him always is on low. He gets very soon pressurized but this time he thinks on his own but little with and thinks of the last time of mistake of him so for this time he goes to Priya and tells her about whole situation to her, makes her convince for getting back her brother to house again. Priya knows the real reason but she is convinced to call him back because she loves her brother a lot and she also wants him in her house so she goes to master's house very early in the morning. Priya knocks the door and master opens the door.

Priya says "Sir where is Deven ,I want to talk to him. "

Master replies "He is inside, come inside angel and say whatever you want to say. "

Priya says "Sorry sir and thank you for your kindness but not this time sir. It's something else so please for next time. "

Master understands the sentence very proper and he guesses why she is here and he counts that and as Deven is her brother and it is her love that has come in his house to bring back the dear one of her so he prefer to stay silent for some second,

After some second he says " I am going to call him. "

Saying this he goes to Deven and tells him about his sister.

Deven immediately runs outside and both the daughter ask him "What happened father? "

Master replies " May be this is a last day of Deven in our house."

The elder one says "Why , is everything o.k outside? "

The younger one says "I won't let him go from here and this is for sure. "

The elder one says "Yah! That's right, we won't let him go from here . We are fully attached with him. His father hats him and at that house, he is never going to be the happy boy like here. This is not fair. "

The master replies "I also don't want that but she is his sister who is calling and her love for him is also the truth. Basically she has the right to let him from here back at her house and I will respect the decision of Deven. I will agree with him whatever he will decide. So now everything will going to depend on him and on his decision. "

Deven at door says" What happen? Why are you here, are you o.k? "

Priya the intelligent girl takes him little away from house and Deven also walks with her.

Priya says "I am here to take you home again at our house. "

"What are you saying?" asks Deven,

Priya says" I am here because father has sent me here to take you home and I also want that. "

Deven says "You know that why he has taken this decision not because he misses me but just due to the words of people that is surrounding in this village. This is not good for him and for his ego.... "

Deven goes emotional and adds "My father is not calling me for his love to me but he is calling me just to shut the mouth of villagers and that is all. "

Priya replies "I know that but I am here to take you to be back with me. "

He says "I am surprise even though you know the real reason, you are here to take me back with you. "

Priya shouts " You stupid boy ,It is not by father's words I am here . I am here just because I love you . I am missing you a lot in that lonely house where nobody is with me. I am missing my brother who had always cared of me. I am alone in that house and you are not ready to feel that. Am I really talking to my brother or this is the boy with the changes? "

He asks "Father is not loving you or not giving much time to you? "

She replies " He loves me and gives me o.k time but that is not enough to me because you are not there and father is never going to be the old one like in past so I am missing you brother . I miss that moment which were with you and in this little time you can't imagine how much I have missed you in that lonely alone empty house without you. "

Deven goes silent so as Priya also for some time and after some seconds Deven says "I am leaving Master's home but on this day, after some hour. Go and I promise, father won't anyway going to take that words anymore about me. "

Priya hugs him with very happy hands and smile is on her face. She goes back to her house.

Deven goes back to his new house and in master's house says" I have decided to leave this house. "

Hiral says" What the rubbish you are talking? "

Sejal says" This is unbelievable. How can you do that ? it is not right. This is not your good decision. "

Hiral says" That stupid man is totally selfish so he is calling you back again to keep people silent and not understanding the situation. "

Master says" Hiral, this is not the right way to talk. "

Hiral says" I am sorry dad but the uncle is really selfish and he is doing this just to make people silent and this is not love."

Sejal adds" Yes Really, if he does love him then why not he has come here and why he has sent his daughter . This shows the real reason and what's the guarantee that he won't torture my brother again so I am not going to have this happen. "

Deven is listening and his attachment with them is pure and he also agrees with them but is silent looking to his master who is thinking,

Master says" I have never forced you for anything and never be so it is your decision and just go with your decision . Don't listen to anybody. Just do whatever you want to do and I will respect your decision always so final decision is up to you and we will support you. "

Hiral says "No, I am not going to for it. You are here and always be so I am not going to let you go. "

Master says "I can understand that and everyone of us want that but just because we want, it is not forcible to someone . One has his one's own life and I want Deven to decide all his decision on own himself. "

Deven is on confusion and he says " I want some time to think so can you all leave me alone for some time? "

Master says "As you wish. "

Deven goes in one of the room of house and locks the door from inside. He is in very much confusion whether to stay here or to leave. He is looking at both sides, one side he feels that loneliness of his sister and love of her to him and on other side, he is seeing the love of one family without any relation and they just want him. Both the sides are good and when he sees the sides with his feelings, he is seeing that the passionate love and the real meaning of love .His mind is thinking all this and has to select the one which is better one, that's what he is doing. After some time with one pack bag with all his things, he comes out of the room and looking at this, the two sister are in shock, The elder one says" Is this your decision? "

Deven remains silent and the little one says "I am going to hate you for this and never will talk to you, "she is saying this with her feelings , the tears are on her eyes and she looks to him with two river.

Deven says" My dear one I am sure you are going to miss me after this decision but I have decided and I am going to miss everybody of you. "

May be the teacher knows this before his decision and he is the one who has never forced any one in his life to be the person who is not independent. He has always believed that person is free whether the decision is right or wrong that is the second thing, the first thing is, person must take his decision by own self and the people can only guide him or her but in last, it must be the decision of an independent without any force so that the person can blame only him or herself not the other one for his or her life's mess. The teacher is the person who is the person with greatness and that's what the boy has seen in his life till now. Deven is on gateway and everybody are there to say the lovely good bye to him and the master gives him the Rupees one hundred and one rupee.

Deven refuses to accept that but the teacher puts that in his hand and says "This is the good bye bless from me and you may not know that but in this rupees the importance is not of the higher one but the importance is of the one rupee coin, that's what our forefathers has said and this one rupee coin is for the good luck and the love and the care and the blessing of mine so take it and be happy always.

After some silence there, Master adds" The things may go against you but you your own self try always to go with yourself and try always not to go against your own self. I hope you will remember this and good bye. "

Hearing the words good luck coin, Deven remembers about The Coin which he has hidden. He hugs all the family members and walks away from there in the way of The coin. He reaches to the tree and after searching for some time, he finds the special coin. He touches that coin and the coin again gives him the powerful feeling, he goes again on his high. It is the way again getting the power and the power gives him the wings. He has decided in master's house that he is going to leave this village and will go somewhere else in any other place. Thinking lot about the situation, he has decided, he has put one notice letter that says" I am sorry sir but I have decided to leave this village because the problem is with me and the ego of my father. I was very happy in this house but thinking about my sister and her love and I have decided to leave . This is the decision I am taking and this very much independently and I am leaving from here because staying here will hurt my father ego again, and again to stay in my father's house is going to be the toughest one for me. I am really not in the position to handle my father's torture again so I am leaving this village and I don't know really where I am going but I will take care of myself and I hope you will also . Tell my sisters about this, hope they will understand this and will respect and love my decision. "

This is a letter in his bedroom. Deven is going and going after taking that coin with him. He is in confusion where to go. He reaches the railway station . The village railway station which is very small and generally the faster train does not stop there. Deven is in station and thinking and thinking so much. He is thinking about the life of him and the love of his sister, mother's care and the hate of his father . He is thinking about the guidance of his master and the short days love of two angel sister. He is thinking all his family and his life and in all this approx two and half hour he passes in at station but he is not aware of time. In village The master and his family is thinking that Deven would have reached his house and on the other side Priya is thinking that he has promised to come in home at evening so he will be there in evening time. Sometimes it happens in everyone's life that the person don't know where to go , what to do and the main question is of what not to do. In that time maximum this happens that person either takes the wrong decision or he gets the wrong with his own self and at that time if anyone takes good decision by own self to his life to make life right and if decision goes in favor of himself that becomes the sign of greatness. Maximum this happens to individual and Deven is the little one who is not aware of this selfish world . What he knows is the only thing in his life is just, all the people are good and if they are not, then they are with their ego . He has seen only love in his life and the much needed guidance of his teacher . The only wrong thing to him is the hate of his father and that is just because of his one incidence in which he has understood the reason of his father's hate so that is all he has found till now is one emotional village . All the person with different nature but with of much needed love. Everybody is ready there to help and help of the kind. May be they are selfish after their help but the help is for sure. He thinks and thinks and many of local trains and mid fast trains stops there and Deven doesn't know anything about this. He only knows is to get in train, one has to buy ticket of the destination but he is very much busy in his thinking that he is unable to think anything else. The one big whistle all of sudden breaks the thinking process of him. What he sees is one train is there and he thinks nothing but gets in and takes one of the seat and again goes sink in thinking process . The train is there because there is some technical issue with that and the train is the fastest one and it generally doesn't stop in such small station . The train with lots of facility and air conditioner. Inside train, it is clean unlike the other one and every one in that is of with their ticket. After some time the train starts again, Deven is in very much in thinking process of his tension so he doesn't realize the first time being seated in air conditioner and he even doesn't have any idea about the train and any station of his range. The ticket checker is in compartment and is checking every ones ticket carefully . Ticket checker is the man with anger and anger is in within him . He is shouting to passenger even for their little mistakes like the leg is not in proper side so the way is not clear ,one little girl is running so it may hurt someone . He is shouting to everybody even without any reason that is because of his personal issue in his life and happiness which he doesn't have find in his life so the frustration of his wife's torture to him is coming with the way of shouts and the anger. Every time he sees a mistake, he remembers his wife scolding to him for his mistake that he often does in his house and the anger face of his wife comes to him and the loud voice to him also so he is not in control of himself by which the anger comes out of him in the face of loud voice.

He goes to one of the passenger and says "Ticket? "

The passenger is reading book and is the dullest one with disorder so he wastes time to show his ticket and the control of Ticket checker goes out and a loud voice comes out of him"

You stupid man. Don't you understand that I have no time and you are taking my time so much ? You such people don't know about the importance of time. "

One side he is saying all these words and in same time he remembers the scold of his wife "You stupid. Don't you know the value of time? you are such a fool of life who doesn't care of time ever. "

The dull person replies " I.... am.... Taking.... Out.... In.... no.... time...., please.... Wait.... For.... Few.... Second....."

The dull person is the slowest one because of his disorder and doing everything very slow. It is his disorder and the person who does not know this reason, often gets angry with him because of his strange and slow process. The ticket checker is the angry one and after seeing this, he goes in upper the level of anger . The dull person has put that ticket in his bag ,first he tries to open his bag and after which he searches the ticket and then he shows that to ticket checker. In all this little work, the dullest person takes three times of one common person that is the reason by which ticket checker gets angry, with stretching his hair the ticket checker says "This is a ticket not a gold that you are keeping like this and wasting everyone's time like this. "

The dull person replies "My....mother....has....told....me.... that....be....aware....of....thives....and....keep....your.... evrything....in....safe....so....i....have....and....my.... mother....has....also....told....me....that....", before the dull person can complete his lines like this, the ticket checker says "keep quiet and please keep quiet. I can't handle this anymore . Please keep your sentence for your next birth. "

The dull person says in excitement" About....next....birth....
my....mother....has....told....me....that,"

The ticket checker very fast keeps his finger on the dull
person's lips and says "Shhhhhhhhhhhhh keep quiet."

The dull person in very attitude manner takes his book which
is just side to him in slow way and starts to read that again.
The ticket checker everyday faces such type of passenger and
even worse than this and after this he faces his wife in house
who tortures him every day for small his mess work. After
facing some other passenger, he comes to Deven. Deven's
cloth is not such type of which he is used to see in that type of
compartment and just by seeing him,

The ticket checker realizes that he has no ticket but just for
formality he asks" Ticket... ticket? "

Deven is in his thinking process with tension and he listens
nothing, he continues in his world.

The ticket checker in loud voice again says "Please ticket. "

Yet not listening Deven , the ticket checker gets angry and
shakes him by his hand through Deven's hand. The shake
is more like twister to Deven, his whole body all of sudden
comes in shock and he sees ticket checker, ticket checker
makes a snap and says "Ticket. "

Deven is in tension and with only thinking ,he is not in
condition to say anything so he heads his head from left to
right for two or three times. Deven is with his only innocent
pain eyes and with very calm body . Looking all this, ticket

checker feels his pain in no time . He sees himself in him and gets emotional. That is what the life has taught him till now but after seeing the corner and helpless Deven, his tears comes out of his eyes without hearing his story. He felts Deven's emotion. He takes him in other room where he asks him about his life but deven is in no position to say anything. Even after some try of ticket checker Deven says nothing about himself. The ticket checker feels his position so he doesn't force him much to say about his past, he understands that his life is of ruin so he asks "Do you know where this train is going? "

Deven heads his head and replies " No. "

"Where you want to go?" the ticket checker asks again,

Deven's face goes reaction less so the ticket checker again feels the answer, the ticket checker says "I want to take you home with me but in my home one witch also lives and I don't want you to get the torture like me in your life so I am ticketing your ticket to next station ,go and handle your life by your own self . May be you will become the one like whom I always wanted to be the "The independent." Just remember that do everything by yourself. Listen to everybody but do as you want to do unlike me who has never done anything of my choice and getting rigid of this always. "

Deven is listening everything and ticket checker adds "From now, you are going to start your new life and going to listen whatever the wish says by making your own decision. "

The ticket checker feeds him his meal and talks to him. The next station comes out. It is Ahmedabad, one of the biggest and developed city of gujarat. It has the biggest railway station with lots of platform in it. The train in ahmedabad's railway station stops for almost 20 to 25 minutes and during this all the time, ticker checker stays with Deven and takes care of him and after the whistle of train, the ticket checker hugs him, byes him in sign and says "Just believe in yourself."

The train goes out. The big railway station is around Deven's eyes. He has never seen such type of any station before and the crowd of such quantity ever in his life. The crowd is so much and everybody is busy with their own work. Everybody is in haste and running here to there to catch the train and for the other work. There are so much people and due to which Deven feels little uncomfortable and suffocation in the place. He does not know where to go ,he does not know what to do, he does not know anything. He stops there almost for one hour without any footstep . After that time and thinking little with, he sees that everyone whoever comes in station is going one way so he also follows the same way. He is climbing the tiles ladder of big size and after following some people and taking the exit way. He comes out of railway station and what he sees the full of voice of vehicle and the drivers of autorikshaws are shouting to every passenger about "where you want to go?"

"sir or madam please come in my auto. "

And the voice of people are surrounding in his ears so much. He has seen like this for the first time . In village he was nothing much of a bird without the wings and the terrific silent nature and all those and he was happy in all that. After seeing that much pollution, he thinks that whether he has done wrong or right by leaving his village? He is tire so much so he sits in footpath and just in front of him one old cut tree is there. That is of 1 feet , the tree has no life in it. Deven opens his bag. He has some clothes in it and he searches more and finds the shoes polisher cream and brush. It is the one which was he had brought for his sister and because she didn't like that so she had put that in his bag and without knowing about it, he had put that in master's house and in last time of village, he just took that bag and his clothes with him so the polisher from that time is still in that bag. He finds the polisher and brush unusable to him so he takes that out of the bag and puts that in that tree and again goes in the process of thinking. The only thing he can do is thinking so he starts his work of thinking again. After some time one man with suit which is the cleanest one and which looks very costly comes to Deven and gives him 5 rupees.

That man says "Hey! boy clean up my shoes and make it like the shining marble. "

Deven sees the 5 rupees note and sees the man with his innocent eyes which has the reflection of his pain. The man sees in his eyes and feels the pain very soon in no time just like the ticket checker. Deven thinks nothing after seeing 5 rupees and takes the rupees and starts . Firstly he tries to open the lid of polisher cream and he doesn't know how to do that but after some efforts, he opens that and after which he takes lot more time in polish. The gentleman immediately realizes that he does not know how to polish. The gentleman is seeing all this with very much patience and smiles. He sits near to Deven and removes his both shoes. Deven is in confusion what is going on, why that person is sitting near to him.

The gentleman asks "Don't you know how to polish shoes? "

Deven very slowly with innocent and with tension in his face replies "I don't know sir. "

The gentleman asks "So why are you here and sitting in such manner that looks like you are the shoe polisher? "

Deven does not look at him and he does not reply to that question. The gentleman does not force him for that.

After some silence, the gentleman says "You don't know how to polish shoes ? It is very simple but for that you must learn to open the polisher cream fast and for that you have to do nothing but to press this lid from one side and it will automatically going to open and after this just take this brush, rub the cream by brush and do like this. "

The gentleman polishes up the shoes in slow motion so that Deven can learn that. The gentleman wears the shoes again and starts walking.

Deven calls him "Excuse me sir. "

The gentleman comes again to him and replies in asking "What my child? "

Deven says "You have done all the work and is going but you haven't taken this rupees of yours, please take it. "

Seeing his honesty, the gentleman thinks for some second and sits again with him.

The gentleman replies "One thing I want to say is today, I am totally free(He is the busy man of his business but for his reason he wants to stay with the boy so he says about his of being free) so take your own time. I am going to take this rupee after you will earn it in some time and till then we can talk. "

Deven finds him very kind and is very impressed with him. He finds him very friendly and all the other are busy in that fast track city.

Deven replies " Why not sir? "

The gentleman says "Please don't call me sir. My name is Ratanbhai and if you like this so call me Ratanbhai or If you want the other option then call me uncle. "

Deven says "O.k uncle. "

After waiting for some minutes, one customer comes to them and asks Deven to polish his shoes. Deven has learnt that very fast so he cleans up the shoes very good so the customer gives him 2 rupees for that which is the real price for polishing the shoes.

Deven asks to Ratanbhai "Uncle, Why you have given me more than the double price against the real price? "

Ratanbhai replies "I have the answer of it but I don't want to give this. I am here so take your own time, I will wait. "

Deven goes little with confusion by that answer but he let that go.

Ratanbhai asks him "Where are you from ? You looks like the stranger to this city. "

"Yes I am. " replies Deven,

Deven finds Ratanbhai very good man .

Ratanbhai asks "So why are you here? "

Deven remains silent. Ratanbhai feels the silent answer so he changes the topic and after some good conversation, Deven automatically starts his story. He finishes some part of story and two customer come to him to make polish their shoes so Deven cleans up the shoes and gets the 4 rupees. Giving that 5 rupees to Ratanbhai, he says" Here it is, please take it uncle. "

Ratanbhai says" I am here with you so why are you in so much hurry to give this to me . You don't like me, you want me to go. "

Deven replies " No uncle , it is my responsibility so I am giving this to you. "

Ratanbhai says "I am here . Just continue your story, don't think so much. "

Deven says "o.k . "

Ratanbhai remains with him for all the day to till evening and hears whole story of him. During this time due to dirt ,sands and pollution his shoes goes dirt again and again so for four time Deven polishes Ratanbhai's shoes and Deven is not aware of this. He is just telling his story and polishing customers shoes. Now it is 7 pm, Deven says "Uncle, now please take this 5 rupees from me. "

Ratanbhai smiles and showing another 3 rupees to him and kindly says" During all this time you have polished my shoes for four time so take this 3 rupees from me. "

Deven smiles and says "I salute you . You are the great one. "

Ratanbhai with lots of hope goes out from there. Deven also walks away from there. Deven is hungry now and he is habitual of his village's pure meal. He sees in street, there are lines of fast food in little small shops. He is not aware of any food items and food items he can see of endless line to line but seeing people eating, his hunger goes on high so he goes in one of the shops and says "I want this what this man is eating. "

The shopkeeper smiles and realizes the being stranger to all this of Deven.

He says " Hey boy! this is a burger and it is of rupees 15. Give me that and I will give you the burger. "

In whole hour of his work, he has earned 70 rupees but he is hungry so much that he is not in time to count all this so Deven says " o.k. "

Deven gives him 15 rupees and after the wait of those long 1 minutes, shopkeeper gives him ready burger. Deven takes burger in his hand and bits on that but the taste of burger he finds very unsuitable for him that he slowly puts that in table and walks away . The shopkeeper is watching all this and the shopkeeper feels that even though he is so much hungry, he left this. How much he has found this burger unsuitable for him . The shopkeeper feels bad for this. After some walk,

Deven spits out all the burger which is on his mouth. He sees every fast food and he is very hungry but what to do, what to eat, he has no solution of it. He is walking and he sees a temple, Lord Shiva temple where the priests of temple are giving normal food to baggers. Without thinking anything, he immediately sits after one bagger. The priest gives him the meal and Deven eats that meal with lots of satisfaction .

He completes that before everyone and asks the priest "Can I take meal one more time? "

The priest kindly replies "Why not, can take as much as you can eat. "

After eating that he washes his hand and that facility is also available with temple, he asks one of the bagger " Aunty for how many days these people will distribute meal like this? "

The bagger lady with very much style replies "Look my son, this is lord Shiva temple and the meal is available for Monday only. "

Deven clearly says" Aunty, I am from small village and is not habitual of these fast food and has liked this temple meal so I am asking you. "

The bagger lady says "Oh! I see. look my son , Every God and goddess are with their own day. Monday is of Lord Shiva, Tuesday is of Lord Hanuman, Wednesday is of incarnation of Lord Krishna so it is the day of lord krishna, Thursday is of lord Saibaba, Friday is of Goddess Santoshi ma, Saturday is of lord Shanidev, Sunday is Of Lord Surya. According to the day, in every temple of the God or Goddess ,priest of that temple distributes the meal in that particular day.

Deven gets very happy hearing this,

He says "Nobody is with me but Lord is with me and he has arranged me my meal . Thank you god for helping me. "

He sleeps in footpath or a ground wherever he finds place to sleep where nobody is with him for some days.

He takes that Coin out of his pocket in every mid night time and says " Hey Lucky coin , why are you not helping me to get out of this ? Why are you not solving my problem ? Help me to find a proper solution for it. "

And After some compliant for some time, he puts that coin in his pocket and sleeps. With new hope in next morning, he walks out from there. According to the day of distribution of meal, he settles himself in that particular temple. For all the day time, he polishes people shoes and in night after eating the meal of temple, he sleeps and some time not. It totally depends on his sleepy mood, if he feels the lonelyness, he talks with that coin in night till the time he is forced to sleep by his mind. He passes two weeks like this. Just walking one temple to another for his meal. He is happy that Lord is helping him and in every night time complaints with The Coin for not helping him . During those fourteen days, he has only lord who supports him and the coin which does not favoring him . That's what he thinks about God and the coin. The memories of village and sisters and the master, this is what he thinks. Every time he thanks God, immediately he complaints to The coin so like this only God and The Coin remains in his life.

In village Rajanbhai is sitting on bricks of well. The total nature is totally white. The sands are white. The trees are white. The leafs of trees are white. The water is white. His clothes are white . Everything around him is white. Rajanbhai is thinking about his wife and his wife comes to him and sits near to him.

she takes his hand in her hand and asks " How are you? "

Rajanbhai replies "Without you, how can you expect to have a nice life of me. "

She kisses him and says "Yah! I am also. And what about our children ? "

Rajan replies " I am taking care a lot much of our daughter. She is smarter than all the other children of this village. She is the cutest and she is the one for whom I am living . She is the hope of me and she is everything to me. "

Jhamkhudi asks "I am asking about our children not about only daughter. "

Rajan replies "You know that, I don't want to talk about him. He has killed you and he is the murderer. "

Jhamkhudi takes him to walk and gives him water to drink and with drinking water, she asks "Do you really think that he has killed me? "

Rajan replies "Yes. "

Jhamkhudi says "O.k, I am going to ask you one toughest question. "

Rajan replies " Go ahead. "

Jhamkhudi asks "Do you love me and do you ever have felt my feelings? "

Rajan smiles and replies "I love you more than how much the water in sea there and about your feelings, I have always realized your every feeling. "

Jhamkhudi with smile says "I love you too and I am agree with you in your first answer but not with the second one. "

Rajan says "Come and hug me and feel the second answer. "

She smiles again.

Rajan with some second gape asks "What's your reason in asking such question? "

Jhamkhudi replies "Because you are wasting my sacrifice in hell. "

Rajan asks "What? "

Jhamkhudi replies "Yes, that's true. I love my children lot more and when I was in position to save his life out of that fire so I have done that. That was my love and sacrifice for him and you are wasting my sacrifice without knowing my feelings. "

She hugs him and says in his ear "If I were on place of my child and if you were in place of mine then I know that you would have gone for the same step as I have done and that is called sacrifice, the sacrifice for loved one. "

Both of them cries and walks, she says "Today my son is in trouble . He is alone. He has no one to support . He is struggling a lot and if my sacrifice is for this then how you have ever felt my feelings ? You have never ever felt my feelings. Just go and have support to him then I will be the happiest one. "

Rajanbhai's dream gets over and he wakes up. He thinks about dream and realized the meaning of his wife's sentence. He for the first time after his wife's death realized the real meaning of her sacrifice that she has made for her son. She was the woman who always had tried hard for her family's prosperity. After realizing his mistake and remembering the days when he had hit his son more than cruel one could being, Rajanbhai slaps himself and by that sound priya also goes wakes up,

She immediately asks " What happen father? "

Rajanbhai remains silent . Priya goes near to him and cleans his tears and again repeats the same question " What happen father? "

Rajanbhai says " I am sorry my dear. "

Priya gets surprise by that answer and asks " Sorry for what?"

Rajanbhai replies " Sorry for making the distance between you and your brother. "

Priya also cries and with that tear she shows how much she has missed her brother in her life.

Rajanbhai sees in eyes of her and adds " What I have done till now , I am the with no answers . This night your mother was there with me and she realized me my sin and everything I did to my son. I am missing him today very much. "

Priya is in tear and with that answer she gets happy and smiles and says " This is good. I am happy that at least you realize your fault and realizing own fault not an easy task and saying sorry is even harder than realizing own fault. "

Rajanbhai hugs her. That is almost of 4:30 am and after that they both not back them to sleep . In morning, Rajanbhai with Priya firstly goes to Master's house. He knocks the door. Sejal opens the door and after seeing the person in front of her, she closes the door again without any word . This time Rajanbhai smiles to own self after feeling the true feeling of Sejal to Deven. He again knocks the door ,

Sejal opens and immediately asks in anger " What you want from this house ? Sorry but don't expect anything and you are going to get nothing not even a good word from us."

Rajanbhai remains silent and Sejal sees his silence . For the first time she founds the gesture of Rajanbhai pure,

She asks "What? "

Rajanbhai says " Sorry my child , I am sorry for everything. "

Master comes there after hearing the words and he says " Please come inside. "

Both of them, Rajanbhai and Priya goes in house . Hiral also gets unhappy after seeing that man in her house.

Rajanbhai sits there and says "I am really sorry for my all

deed because of which you got distance from Deven. Today I have realized my fault so I am here. "

Master says "Finally the day is good for you as you have realized. "

Priya says " Yes sir, finally the day is here . He has realized it. I am very happy. "

Rajanbhai says " I don't know where he is and what I am going to do for his search but it is sure that till I won't find him , I am not going to take a rest and that is for sure. "

In city, In those two weeks Deven has not spent his any money else than to purchase shoe polisher and brush. He has saved rupees 740 rupees. It is the some kind of magic that Deven has had used that much polisher and still he is doing that and he has not purchased more than two times . That is strange to him but he never has noticed that. He has eaten as per the distribution process of temple. After those longest two weeks, Deven is outside temple doing his polishing work. He is looking to shoes with only attention and polishing them, one man comes to him from a car and asks "So how you are here? "

Deven sees him and gets surprised by that, his tears automatically comes out of his eyes after seeing someone known in that city.

Deven says with tears and smile "It is a long story. "

Ratanbhai also smiles and says "I am free again for whole day. "

Ratanbhai sits near to him. Deven starts his two weeks story and the only thing he doesn't tell to him is about the coin else he tells him everything. Deven completes his two weeks story in two hour like before.

Ratanbhai says "Pack your bag, you are coming with me and will work in my factory. "

Deven without thinking anything immediately packs his bag and sits in car and says "Oh! Wow, from inside this car looks like one little house. "

Ratanbhai smiles and drives him to his factory where he provides him one room to live and all the facility of cooking. He teaches him gas starting process and all the cooking process. Deven learns that very soon in some hour. Deven is happy and he knows the cooking very well. He makes rice, dal and vegetables to eat and serves to Ratanbhai.

Ratanbhai eats and says "Wow! Wonderful, you are very good in cooking. "

Deven replies "My sister also thinks same. "

After having his meal Ratanbhai asks him to have a rest. Next day, he teaches him the working process of his company and shows him the production of clothes for which they are famous for . Ratanbhai asks him to work there as a labour and learn all the work as early as possible.

One day Ratanbhai decides to travel the good place and for that from his house he decides to explain the main thing about the life. He is so much in affection with Deven. This is the day when he is going very smooth .By his behavior now it is clear that he is showing his attachment for that. He is for the maximum time remains in factory to have time with Deven. From house he reaches to Factory.

Ratanbhai says to Deven " Today I am planning to visit some good place of Ahmedabad , would you like to come?

Deven replies without any hesitation " Why not, this is very good idea." he smiles.

Ratanbhai says" Then come and join me."

Deven sits in a car and Ratanbhai starts the car.

Ratanbhai asks " Do you like music?"

Deven replies " I have never had heard song else than some folk song."

Ratanbhai asks " Then what was your source of enjoying and the source of some other villagers in your village?"

Deven replies" As a child I was just there with some playing the local childhood friends and that was the play may be I am going to miss for my life. The old person of my village, great,great and the great."

Ratanbhai asks in surprise " Why , What did they do?

Deven smiles and replies " When I was in my village what I had seen is very great to me and strange too. All old men maximum were there with retirement of their work as their son had had taken all the responsibility and what was the job of them was to make every evening some meeting in particular place and in that place it was necessary to come all the old men and even young men. They got together and discuss some serious issue like problem of road and water and other issue. Maximum time they had political issue and that was too with seriousness in line totally and that was the very strange thing. The political view point of everyone was so aggressive and even sometimes they were in position to fight with each other if some opposed the other one and I was always wondering why they were quarrelling with each other. The progress of village was known to everyone how that was going but they were favoring particular cast wise leader. The thing of topic was taken by them always on serious mode. The day of village was in real I think that was the great day. The day was heavily on my poor side and very strong to all my love and I had spent the day. (Ratanbhai sees him with love and smiles) why are you smiling uncle?"

Ratanbhai says "Dear, you are very innocent and cute. You continue please."

Deven says " I really don't know anything about innocent."

After some silent Deven speaks up" The action for the work of my ideology is perhaps not for everyone but the action for the love of my ideology is always for all."

"Do you think it's really you mean it what you have just said" asks Ratanbhai in his very calm way.

"Yeah but not for every time but surely for maximum time " Deven replies.

Deven asks " Uncle tell me where is aunty or are you still unmarried."

Immediately after hearing the word about his wife, he gets emotional and takes some second to recover. Deven sees all this and sees little tear in his eyes. To avoid this answer Ratanbhai asks " Do you like to eat ice-cream ,if yes then of which flavor?"

Devens with smile replies " Saying it frankly, I don't know anything about this . I have never eaten ice-cream but always heard of that and seen other eating so I don't know any flavor of any ice-cream."

" O.k my son I will get you the best flavor of it after reaching the garden we are going to " says Ratanbhai.

They reach the garden where As per his promise, Ratanbhai buys ice-cream and after eating that they both start to play in garden. After so much time Ratanbhai is enjoying the moment of his life and he is playing the game of little small boy and forgets all about his past. That is the moment what is needed by him and he gets more attachment to Deven. After playing in garden ,they go for a movie and some temples too. The plan is of Ratanbhai is of just of some hour but he involves with Deven in enjoying the day so much that he forgets about the time for whole day and makes his day of his life in his way like he was used to some years ago.

Deven completes three months working there and he is happy. As he is child and his expenses are less so he has saved more than any one. One day when he is working, Ratanbhai comes to him and takes him in his office room,

Ratanbhai says "I am happy with your work and I am unhappy with your work too. "

Deven gets in little surprise, he doesn't say any word but reacts as his eyes are asking why unhappy?

Ratanbhai says "I know you want to know the reason of my unhappiness, Come and have sit."

Deven sits in sofa and Ratanbhai takes a chair and sits near to him.

Ratanbhai says "I have seen that you are working for last three months here very hard even working overtime . I am happy with your hard work but in the same time I am unhappy with your hard work. "

Deven gets confuse, Ratanbhai adds "Confuse my boy, confuse. Being the little lazy is not bad . Just think that if the car inventor was happy with his walking and not being the lazy to sit comfortably and just drive down then how we could have this facility in this time and there are lots of example like this. All I want to say is being the habitual of anything in excess is always a problem . Habitual of getting totally hard working man is also wrong and vice versa so with your hard working attitude think about being little lazy and create your creative idea about the factory's work so that we can have more facility here. "

Deven smiles. Ratanbhai knows that he has understood the idea so he walks away out of room and after thinking for some time Deven also goes out outside. In only eight month after the advice of Ratanbhai, Deven gives Ratanbhai such a good idea which Ratanbhai never had.

One day when Deven is in tea stall to sip tea , one man comes to him and puts his hand in Deven's shoulder. What Deven sees a long hairy, long moustache and long bear man. The man with very much dirt in cloth. His face is very much unclean . Deven is in confusion who is he?

The man says " I am your father , don't you remember? "

Deven gets very much shock and Deven stands up . His father hugs him. Deven is in shock that how he is like this totally a mess man.

Rajan says "My boy, I am sorry for what I have done to you . I have realized my mistake . I have realized my fault so please forgive me and come with me. "

Deven asks " Is Priya o.k? "

His father replies "Yes, she is o.k. "

Rajan repeats "I am sorry my son. "

Deven says "Please father don't say again . I have always loved you a lot but it is not possible for me to go with you . I am happy here. "

Rajanbhai tries more to convinced Deven but Deven is not ready to come with him. Deven walks away in his factory.

Rajan stands there and smiles and says "For the first time I have seen myself into you and how I have behaved with you. You have behaved less to me than that. " With smile in his face he also walks away from there.

After one hour Ratanbhai comes to Deven and says "Deven come with me , I want to talk to you. "

Deven follows him , Ratanbhai says " See this paper , all you have to do is to sign this. "

Deven asks " What is this and what it is all about? "

Ratanbhai replies calmly "I am adopting you . This paper is all about that, just sign it. "

Deven goes in tears and hugs him, both of them are in tears,

Deven says "Why suddenly? "

Ratanbhai replies " It is never a sudden . You don't know two years before I met you, my wife and my daughter were died in one car accident . I was also in car but had found myself safe in hospital after some days . Doctors were surprised and called me living man just because of miracle. I had asked god every time why he had saved me? I was alone for all that time and was in pain. My memories were always calling my wife and daughter. I had asked god to take me with him and I even had tried some suicide attempts. Six month before I met you , doctor informed me that I had a cancer , I was the happiest one after hearing that report. I remember when I was happy after hearing the cancer news, all doctors were in very much surprised and after seeing their faces I laughs even loud. Then the day when I saw you for the first time you were in very much tension ,heading your head down. I wanted to see your face so I made a excuse of shoe polish after seeing the polisher in front of you. For the first time when I saw your face that reminded me of my family, the daughter of me. I found the tension , I realized your pain after hearing your past and at that night when I was in home I had just thought of you and no one else. For two days that continued, I decided to adopt you. The third day I went to the railway station to find you but you were not there and had found you after twelve days of that day. I was happy but just not told the decision of adoption to you at that time . I wanted to make an emotional attachment relationship before the adoption just to convince you about the adoption as you would have never agreed for the adoption if I would have told at that time so I took my time and I am telling you about my decision today, are you agree? "

Deven cries so as his new father. His new father hugs him and the tears are falling and falling. At that time the emotional attachment of Ratanbhai and Deven gets new relationship with new feelings. Deven and Ratanbhai two of sad past gets each other to start their new way this day and they are the happiest person of this day. Ratanbhai makes a time to make a final relation with Deven and it is a quality of him that makes him the great person always.

Next day in the morning when Deven is working in his factory, the security guard comes to him and says " Somebody is looking for you out side. "

Deven says " Who? "

The guard replies " I don't know. "

Deven walks with him outside the factory and sees his father with his sister .

He takes them in his room and says "I have told you that I don't want to come with you but you are again here. "

His father cries and says "I am really sorry my son . Please forgive me and include me again in your life. "

"Please father, I don't want this. Please don't force me. " replies Deven,

Rajan tries and Deven avoids . All this is happening and Priya is seeing all this without any word. Rajan is trying very hard but Deven is in his way. Priya takes a drink of water and drinks, holds Deven's hand and says "You don't want then it's o.k but we have some rights that I am going to complete and you have to listen that. "

Deven looks to her , his father also sits calmly,

Priya says "You are saying that you don't want him again in your life. That's o.k but you are doing the same mistake as has been done by him before. You don't know but when father has realized his mistake, he immediately sold his shop and house and after giving me to the teacher's house for my safety and searched you. He searched you for the last eleven months continuously. Look at him , look his condition . His condition says everything to you, how he has felt everything and how much he has searched you. Many of time he would have not eaten anything that you can see by his body condition and it is his love and realization. He searched you in every near village , every other city why because he realizes his mistake. Everyone in this world makes mistake , he has too and you are not forgiving him and doing the same mistake as he has done to you . So the choice is yours. " Everybody in that room goes in tears.

After twenty years, today Deven is now 29. He is in list of top 10 businessmen in india. He is the number one richest man below 30 in the world. Like his mother had dream off always that one day they will be above the need of necessity. Deven has a big house which is superb than superb with all kind of facility. He is a busy man but he is the man who has always time for his family. He believes in living life with family members. Rajanbhai a man who is busy in himself . Now he plays chess always whenever he gets time otherwise he is a busy man in his NGO for little small orphan children. He plays with children like never before he has done. He has suffered in his childhood so remembering all that now he is living his life and giving all the time to children. The intelligent girl Priya who is now of 25 , helps his brother in business as a vice president of company . Again she is small for all this but she is above all in mind and IQ . She has completed her MBA in Harvard University with always number one . She is the girl who has surpassed Mr. genius Albert Einstein in IQ level test by big margin. Everybody in her office respects her for all her achievement. Everybody knows her power and she is the girl who is the best in the world with her capacity. She has joined her company just before two years but with her intelligent decision, she has got everything. She is the one who is even above her brother in case of respect. If business has any problem, she is available to solve that. The only thing which Deven has more is polite. He is very calm and cool. One day it is a big business meeting and Priya is giving her presentation, Deven is looking at her and he is not concentrating in the words of her. Priya is also noticing that but she avoids that till the meeting ends.

After meeting she goes in his cabin and asks "Is there any problem with you? "

Deven doesn't reply to her .

She says " I am repeating , Is there any problem with you? "

Deven says "Have a sit. "

She sits and he adds "This is the same question which I want to ask you ? "

Priya understands what he is talking about but just to show him like being the unknown, she asks "What? "

Deven says "Don't try that, I have noticed that now days your behavior is little strange. You are giving less time to us and even to business which is your favorite, may I know why? "

she says with little smile "Brother this is not like this , you are thinking wrong. The matter is hmmmmm …… I mean to say the matter is not like this. "

Deven gets up and puts his hand in her shoulder and says "Relax, after so many years I have seen you like this . The last time when I have seen is I don't remember. "

Priya says "You got me . The matter is I am in love with someone. "

Deven asks in surprise "Oh really! Who is that lucky one? "

Priya says "He is not lucky but I feel like I am the lucky one. "

Deven says " Oh really! Who is he? "

Priya says "His name is Vicky. "

Deven says "Asks him to meet me in our house this Sunday in morning at 6:30 am. "

Priya happily replies "I will . I love you brother."

The next day, that is the day of Friday when Deven starts his morning by waking up early in the morning. That is the day which is very important for the business as he has an important agreement deal with the main most powerful industry of Japan Aruku pvt. Ltd. It is the day by which sunshine pvt. Ltd. of india is going to make the biggest deal by which Deven and his Sunshine pvt. Ltd. can make the establishment of root to first time in the Japan. The day is very very suffocate. His mind has the think about the deal and he is very much confidence about the success of that deal so he is making his every step by thinking about the deal. The other reason of his being confidence that type is that he knows that he has his lucky coin and if one has that type of lucky coin , what needs else to be confident. After completing his routine work and all that, he goes to breakfast table and there in table already is Priya .

Priya says" Today is a big day for us, isn't it brother?"

Deven says " Yes it is. This is very special day for our business as we have waited for this time to come more than the time.

Priya says " We have prepared everything of our best and this is what we have to represent to get the collaboration and if we get success in this, we will definitely going to make the maximum of our profit."

Deven says " Yeah ! And by which we will get the maximum of our level and we will get the transaction of best. The main thing is after today the value of our goodwill is surely going to increase."

Priya says " Surely , we are ready 100%."

Outside in garden Rajanbhai and his friend after the morning walk are sitting on table.

All of sudden Rajanbhai screams " Deven come here and help me."

Deven and Priya listens that and runs to outside. In the garden Rajanbhai is handling his friend who got heart attack.

Deven asks" What happened?"

Rajanbhai replies " We were talking and all of sudden he gets heart attack."

Priya says " Don't worry, I am taking my car till than just handle him."

Priya works fast to get her car, Deven raises Rajanbhai's friend and puts in car. They all take him to hospital where after some treatment doctor comes to Deven.

Deven asks " Is he o.k?"

Doctor replies "Yeah! He is . That was the minor heart attack. You did good nice that you took him very fast. Sometimes consuming time can make difference.

Deven's mobile rings and Deven receives " Tell me."

The secretary of office says " Where are you sir ? The managing directors of Aruku is on their way and they will get here very soon."

Deven says " Oh! I forgot about that . We will be there in no time."

Secretary says " O.k sir."

Deven in sign calls Priya and when she comes near, he says "Doctor said Uncle is o.k and we are getting late for office. We should depart."

Priya says " O.k why not?"

Priya says to his father" Everything is o.k now. if you need any help, contact us . We are getting late for office so we are going."

Rajanbhai says" All the best."

They reach in office in 15 minutes and after 6 minutes of that the Managing Directors of Aruku pvt. Ltd. Reaches in office. Deven and his sister welcomes them. They take them in Rest room where they are given some time to rest. Deven is preparing for his words and how to present all his deal at best level to get the deal. In middle of that Deven touches his pocket to touch the THE COIN but that is not in his pocket as he has forgotten to take that in welter matter of uncle. Deven is also going in the way of Maheshbhai. Deven is also now in intoxication of THE COIN. He whenever there is big deal to his business, he takes that COIN in his pocket to take the advantage of luck but today he forgets in haste. Now he is feeling very low in his confidence. He is in his cabin and thinking about how to face that situation. This is the first time when he is without his COIN in his big agreement deal and he doesn't know what to do. Even though he has prepared very hard every small thing about the deal so that they can get the deal in their favor but he is feeling very low on his esteem and his confidence is going on a smooth ground level of building from where he is seeing no way to come again and raise himself. His brain is in confusion about the matter of fact and his brain and every organ of his body with his brain is making noise in his brain so he gets headache by that. He again and again drinks water to keep himself calm down but he is unable to do that.

The secretary comes to his cabin and says " Sir meeting is ready to start."

Deven says " You go , I will be there in few seconds."

The secretary says " o.k sir."

After some seconds, he comes out from his cabin to attend the meeting. It is pre decided that Deven is going to represent all the things. Deven enters in board meeting room and sits silently in his chair. All the other staff and the managing directors of Aruku pvt.ltd.also enters. After some starting process by staff members of Sunshine pvt. Ltd. it is the time of Deven to represent all the matters to all the members but Deven is in his thought.

Priya says " Where are you Brother? It's your time."

Deven is fearing of losing the deal just because he has no lucky COIN with him.

Deven says " Priya , Go and represent the deal and its every prospect."

Priya is in surprise but she shows her surprise not more than 2 seconds and behaves in normal manner again.

Priya says to all " Now I am going to present everything to you."

Every members of that room thinks that it is the love of a brother to his sister so he is giving this responsibility to her. Priya doesn't know the real reason but she knows her brother and that is not the matter of love and she knows that reason surely. Priya is sharp enough to handle this type of situation all of sudden. She represents everything more accurate and in 100% confidence with her intelligence. She represents and after meeting the managing directors of Aruku pvt.ltd is so impressed that they confirm their deal. Everyone is happy in office and Deven is also showing his happiness but from inside he is feeling some emptiness. He is thinking that just by forgetting the lucky coin why he is feeling very low in his himself. He is thinking about all the thinks and that is very hard to understand for him. His mind is asking again and again the same question but in a different manner.

Priya asks him" What is going? can you tell that to me?"

Deven replies " Nothing, All is well now and you did very good job."

Priya says " This is not done . I am asking the why question?"

But in mid of that conversation , some members come there and interrupt them.

One staff man says " Congrats mam! You did a very nice job today."

Priya replies " Thanks."

The other one says" Credit goes to Deven sir. It was pre-decided that all representation would be given by sir but in last time sir changed his mind and trusted to his sister and result is in our favor .Very nice job done by you sir."

Priya is not convinced with that but to avoid that she says " Yeah! That's true."

Deven is answerless at that time. He is in confusion. His face is silent. The whole day of him he undergo like that. He is in his cabin and is silent for continuous. Office our goes and everybody leaves office.

Priya goes in Deven's cabin and asks him "Let's go brother, where are you?"

Deven in very slow voice answers "I am going to be late. I have some other work, you just go."

Priya asks in surprise " Are you sure?"

Deven replies " Yes, sure."

Priya says "O.k brother , I am going."

Saying that Priya goes and Deven remains in his cabin.

From his cabin he calls his driver, driver was in his room downside the building and he receives the the call " Hello uncle" Says Deven.

Driver says " Yes son , I am just coming with the car in few seconds."

Deven says " Hello uncle firstly listen to me."

Driver says "Yes son."

Deven says in his calm voice " I am here and I don't know how much time it will take to complete myself so you can go."

Driver says " If you ask, I can stay here."

Deven says " No, no need of that , you can go. I will adjust myself, you can go."

Driver says " O.k son."

What Deven is in need is silent. By today's incident he is not in his proper good situation. He removes his suit in that cabin and also removes his in shirt. He is doing that but all in very much slow activation. After that he remains in his cabin alone for more than 3 our silently just by thinking about the fact . Why he is feeling so much loneliness and emptiness about himself and what is his situation in real. He asks to himself about whether he is going so much dependent and all that. It is now 10 o clock in office clock so Deven decides to go home but he takes that decision very hardly. He goes down side the building by walk and his office is in tenth floor of building but he doesn't realize that he has for the first time downs the office by walk. In the main gate of office, there are so many taxis but he decides to walk. He is walking and walking continuously without any feeling for anything. He walks in a road and reaches in one silent road where there are nobody but he walks without any feelings. All of sudden he listens one voice. There is one old man and two persons are snatching his money and he is shouting for help. The two has targeted the good target as he is old and can't do much to defend.

The Old man shouts " Help ,please help."

Deven hears his voice and the old man also sees Deven.

The old man says "Hey! Boy, please help me."

One of the two says" Hey! man just stay out of this, this is not your matter."

The other one says " You get lost."

Deven is looking at that and he is feeling very low in his confidence to handle that. Deven gets fear and so much fear to go and help the old man. The two men get success and take all the money of that old man.

The one man says " He is looking also good healthier moneywise. Let's see."

The other one says "This money is enough to pass some days. Before somebody will come, we have to take our path." and they run away.

Deven is seeing all that and after that, Deven goes to that old man.

Deven asks " Are you o.k?"

The old man says " That two man took my whole amount. I was in very much need of that amount." The old man cries.

Deven says " I have money. I can help you. Don't bother about the money."

Deven takes his money from his pocket and gives to the old man. The money is more than the two man took away.

Deven says " Take this."

The old man says in anger " Why do you want to help me now. When there was real time to help me , you didn't. You are so young and if you would have tried to help me then surely you would have. Now you are giving me this . I don't need your help. That was my money and this is not. Keep this with you."

Deven feels again very low in himself and says " But…"

The old man says " I am in need of money but I really don't need your money. Now I don't need your any help." Saying this the old man stands and walks to his way.

Deven is thinking. What all is going on? Why he is fearing ? Why didn't he help the old man? If Deven would have tried, he would have got success to help the old man but in real he is going very much habitual of the coin and The COIN has transacted the fear in Deven's mind. After that Deven reaches his house after walking for half an hour where he directly goes to his bedroom and sleeps without eating.

Sunday in Deven's house early morning at 6:15 am rings the phone,

Deven receives and says "Hello,"

Says the gatekeeper "Sorry to disturb you sir but here is one man saying his name is Vicky and he is here to meet you and have an appointment. "

Deven says " Let him in. "

Deven comes outside the house in garden so as Priya does. Rajanbhai is already there sipping his green tea and Priya asks Vicky to have a sit with them in garden to have green tea.

Deven asks "So Vicky what you do? "

Vicky kindly replies "I am an owner of little small cafe. "

Priya says " Brother we met in his cafe . His coffee is very good. "

Deven smiles and says "Vicky I would like to taste that. "

Vicky says " Why not sir. "

They drink their tea and Deven says " Priya, I think you know more of him but I want to know him more so please leave us alone. "

Priya says "That's cool. I am sure you are going to like him. "

Deven says with smile "I have already. "

Priya says " O.k I am going for my jogging. "

Rajanbhai also after having his green tea and meeting with Vicky goes to his NGO.

After Priya goes,

Deven says "Tell me more about yourself but don't take it like interview or test. it is just for my knowledge. I know if she has selected you means you are already pass in all. "

Vicky smiles and says "My name is Vivek Maheshbhai Patel in short people call me Vicky. Do you ever have heard about Maheshbhai the businessman , I am his son. "

Devens gets shock "Are you the same one ? Maheshbhai was the great in his business. "

Vivek says " Yes I am. "

Deven says "I know about him, I have read. "

After some silent seconds,

Deven adds "That much big business and went in insolvency. Nobody has ever believed that one . Do you know the reason?"

Vivek again smiles and replies "I know . It was something which was unbelievable to anyone. "

Deven says "Really! tell me. May be I am going to believe. "

Vivek says "I have told this only to Priya. "

Deven says " You can trust me too. "

Vivek after making another cup of green tea says "It was all because of me and that The Coin. "

Deven immediately asks " The Coin , which Coin? "

Vivek says "The lucky coin , always shining lucky coin. "

Deven gets idea that he is talking about which coin but to confirm he calmly asks "May I know more? "

VIvek replies "The coin , the shining coin in which one side there was a symbol of star and other side it had The English capital word T . I exactly remember that. "

Deven gets up with some surprise.

Vivek says "What happen sir? "

Deven says" Nothing, just come with me inside. "

Vivek follows him and Deven takes him to his bedroom where he opens a small box and says "Look into it, is it? "

Vivek sees and says "I can't believe this really. "

Vivek is in surprise to see that coin again .

Vivek adds " I can't believe this that I am seeing this coin in my life again."

He remembers some of his past and goes emotional.

After some seconds silent, Deven says "The hardest word I am saying in my life is take this with you, you are the real owner of this. "

Vivek says "No , I can't. "

Deven asks "Why? why not? You are the real owner of it so why not? "

Vivek says "I am not, you don't know the history of it. It was gifted by one of the british general to my forefather for his serve to him. "

Deven says " But you are the one. "

Vivek says " Please sir have sit , I want to say more. "

Deven sits ,

Vivek asks " Are you the one who has caught this coin? "

Deven says " Yes I am. "

Vivek says " We were the richest family of that time. We had all the facility of that time. My father loved me more than any one. My mother was there always to me with lots of love. The only problem with my family was, we were the family in which my father didn't talk to my mother and my mother didn't talk to my father due to some misunderstanding of big reason. I was the only connection between them for whom they were living together. Many of times I had seen that my mother had tried to fill some gape with some communication but my father didn't respond to that but due to that they had never ever had made me felt of their love less to me. After my birthday celebration, we met accident so my father decided to visit Temple Balaram places and that was my idea of to visit there by local train. I was the happiest one in that local train and in that excitement I had thrown this coin to you which was I had took without the knowledge of my father from his secret room. I was not aware of that even in temple where we were enjoying a lot. My father was really the man who had always trusted this coin more than anyone. In that temple when I was enjoying in water by feeding to fish , all of sudden I realized the coin was missing. I was very tensed at that time and after some flash back I realized that I had thrown this in that bridge to you . I was very upset after that and very much in tension, how to tell my father about that ? After that visit, my father went to Austria for his official meeting and deals and he was there almost for 1 month. After few days of completion of that month, one night my father was in tension and he was calling someone and saying how could this be happened? he was saying that his company got a big loss in particular one state . I saw him with lots of tension in his face. I went to him.

I was nervous but I said " Father I want to say something to you."

He replied to me in happy manner even though he was tensed" My son you are always allowed to tell me anything. Tell me, I am always for you here ,there and everywhere".

I was in confusion how to tell my father about the worst bad sentence of his life and so I was fearing of that and hesitation was on my face. My father came to me one step ahead, he sat on his knee,

He said to me with love " My dear son , the dearest to me, tell me whatever you want to say", he rubbed my head.

I got convinced by his way of rubbing my head and with his voice so by some courage I said" Father the day we went to Balaram temple before that I took that the lucky coin from your special room and I am really sorry to say but in excitement I threw that to the children who were bagging downside the train."

My father slept me immediately in anger. That was the first time when he had hit me . At that time I didn't understand the anger of him to me of so much but today I understand that very well. I cried a lot in that night. After some days when everything was going bad and my father was on shock. That was the time when the fall of the Patel industries started. My father started to feel helpless. After that whenever I saw him, he was always on tension. He was not like the before one father. Loss of coin had affected so much in his life. I also started to feel bad so I decided to talk to my mother and my mother had also seen him like this for the first time . I went to her in her room and stood near door and tears were on my eyes.

My mother came to me and asked "Why are you crying? what happened?"

I told her everything what had happened. I found that even my mother was not aware of that coin. It seemed that she had heard about that coin for the first time. My mother took me to my father.

He was drinking.

She said " You don't talk to me that is else matter but you have slept my son, it is not done and the secret you have hidden from me that is not good. You even didn't tell me all this in the beginning of our marriage life and now you are doing even worse. Feel yourself, that was just a coin, Why are you loosing yourself just because of that coin?"

My father said "You keep quiet, I don't want to talk to you " he said in much anger.

But this time she was not even ready to listen to him , She said "Shouting at me doesn't really mean you are right " she told this in very unusual way. And added "If you really feel that was the luckiest coin , no one disagree with you but now that was past and you have to recover from it as early as possible otherwise it could cover whole your tree."

My father was the man who was told by her that he didn't talk to her that was matter of her relationship without which he was good on his confidence condition but that secret he had hidden from her and now totally depending on it and the control of him was over to that coin and was thinking always about that which had totally lowered his confidence . She tried very hard to convince him to be confident and she believed in his work so much that he could do even without that coin but my father was depended so much to This coin.

He said very much in anger " I don't want to talk to any of you. You just get lost. I want to be alone so leave me alone."

After some days, I heard from somewhere that my father was losing everything and he was not trying his best to recover. He didn't talk to me for much than Six month. One night when I was in my room with lots of tension in my face about my father. He came to me slowly.

He said much emotionally like he had lots of depression in him yet love to me " My son , I am really sorry for that night when I had slapped you. I love you very much . When I had slapped you that night after which I didn't sleep for 3 days as if I was feeling much the worst than ever I had felt (he started crying). I am sorry. You are my charm without you I can't imagine my world so please come to me and hug me .

I also started to cry and in crying I said " No dad, don't be sorry ,I am sorry for making you lonely. I did big mistake. I didn't care much and lost your luck. Please forgive me."

I knew that my father loved me more than anyone but that night what I had seen was the greatest deep sea on his face and I realized what was the meaning of love and care in this world. I went to him and he hugged me. At that night we both were crying and crying all night. For the all night he was caring me again and again and was saying sorry to me again and again. That night was the biggest memory of my father ever to me. I had seen that my father was absolutely dependent of that coin and without that he had lose his confidence and on the other side my father's business was going and going in opposite direction of up. Everybody had left us. Everybody whom we wished to support us, were going away from us. My father's every company went down in insolvency in that little time of some years and that was unbelievable to anyone but it is true because of this lucky coin. We were forced to live in small house with no money in our hand. My father had given up and he was not ready to try to restart as restarting is not easy task to everyone. That's common thing in his mind that starting again was going to be much difficult than ever as he had not had his lucky coin. After that so much facility with us and we were in that position at that time that we were struggling even for necessaries of life. The only hope in my family was my mother who had always tried to get up. During that time, she was the sole earner who had started life with job again. During that time, she had proven her love to my father. During that time my father realized that he was wrong in his past for not to talk with her and not to feel her love to him. What I was seeing at that time was my father was slowly realizing his mistake about his faith in his wife but only showing with his gesture and didn't tell her till . My mother had also realized that and she was happy in that. She had given me the love . Some people are made for with never give up thought and my mother is one of them. During that time she made the difference in our house with her thoughts otherwise the position would have gone even miser than one can think. The only think I loved about that time was that during that time, my father and my mother got each other.

After a year, one day my father catch my mother's hand and said " Sorry, Sorry for not trusting you, Really sorry ."

My mother got touched by that touch and she said " I am always with you and going to always forever ."

With the love and encouragement by her, he started to live with some happy moment. He never got that much confidence so that he can start to earn for family again. Me and my mother had also accepted him like that. We wanted just to make my father happy and live his life again. My father started to be happy but he was getting sick from inside day by day. He made his those days lovely with his family. My mother also showed best love to him. We struggled almost for 6 years and after which my mother got some good salary that we could start at least our life as a middle class family of india and after two year of that my father died because of his ill health. I remember the last word, he told me "Never ever be the person depending on lucky things. "

I promised him because I knew why he was saying that. My mother was the person who got herself badly affected much than anyone to crying mode that she was there and she was there with continues in tears for almost one week non-stop. The almost one week which was the heaviest to my mother and at that time I was the one who had seen her continuously crying and at that time I was in confusion whether she is going to recover ever or not. After that longest week of her life, she stood up again just because of me to care me again so that I could make my life. With my mother's support, I have completed my graduation in B.B.A and after working three years as an assistant manager, I started my own cafe with some loan . I met Priya for the first time in my cafe. "

Deven says " Yes, your father was right . We are the people who are always searching for some lucky thing and if that is found, we care for that and depend on that. I am also the same. Whatever I am , whatever I have got is just because of this coin. I have realized from the first day of it that it has always given the luck factor to me. We were of family with very poor background and in my childhood I was the dare boy who had never ever had fear of anything. When I got this coin, my good days started and when I came here from the village, luck was with me in train, railway station. Railway station where I found the great man of my life, my new father who had adopted me after giving me the chance of 11 month as he wanted the attachment relation between us. When I was here, nobody was in support of me. I traveled two longest week of my life with the support of god and at that time I thought the coin was not helping me so I started to throw my frustration to it and today I am realizing that if I would not have thrown my frustration to it, May be I would be the other anger man. My new father who taught me the realization of life in very short time. When my real father and sister came to me and convinced me to be the village boy again, at that time my new father had stopped me and convinced my sister and father to live with him like a family. He died after 5 years of that because of cancer. He was the fighter man in real.

He had fought with cancer for more than 66 months no one ever could have done before and always had said " I am living and fighting with this, just because of you. I want to live more for you. I want to love you forever."

During that time I had learned so many and the best thing of my life which I am following yet. The success of being the richest youngest businessman is due to this coin but not without him. If you have something like this coin then who want more than this . During all this year ,this coin has supported me and this has given me the opportunity every time to take and make my world the finest. I have never told to anybody about this else than you because you know already about this. The only thing I have got bad from this coin is fear, fear of losing it. It has suck my good habit of be the bold man. I have realized that this coin gives you the luck but sucks your ability of work . You are totally going to depend on this and depending on something like this is very bad to anybody like your father and me also. My godfather Ratanbhai had always told the good lesson to me of not being the dependent on anything more of excess. "

Vivek asks " Sometimes I think all about the past in one role and today I am thinking, Why all this to us ? I find difficult to find this."

Deven says " Yes the past, all the lesson we learn are from our past and what I have learnt is fear comes to us in whatever way is never good for us."

Vivek says " The point is very much right."

Deven asks " Much in clear and real way?"

Vivek replies " Yeah."

Deven says" Moreover, much heavier word is fear comes to us and any of which stays with us for long time that is the most dangerous thing in our life."

Vivek says" That's what fear is all about. Absolutely 100% correct."

After silence for some second,

Vivek says "May be the another point is I imagine a world where luck must be circulated to everybody who needs that, not to them who have already got so many with it with such type of things like this coin. "

Deven says "What you want to say? "

Vivek replies "I am just supposing that the capital T is for Try, may be it want to say don't be the man depending totally on me and try yourself also. "

Deven says "I think you are right. This coin is saying this itself and it is the message of it. Whoever had realized this had given to another person like that general to your forefather. "

Vivek smiles and says "But my forefathers didn't realize it and It becomes our property, hell property. In last I had given this to you just by co-incidence. "

Deven says "This coin is saying, change my owner after your need will complete. "

Vivek again smiles and says "Yeah ! but only the need of your need not more than the need of your need."

Deven also smiles and makes his body as per Vivek's sentence.

Vivek says "So what to do now. "

Deven says "If we come to this very nice of it then why not to do this. "

Vivek asks " What?"

Deven says " Why not to start the search of next the needy owner from today, from now?"

Vivek says "How you are going to find that the person you are giving it is the needy one of it really. "

Vivek smiles and adds " Like I had found. "

Deven also smiles and says " Yeah! That's the hard one to answer. Why not start today ? let's travel to some needy place and find someone if we can today. "

Vivek asks "Are you sure, the person you will find for it is going to give it to another man after his completion of bad time to somebody else for its luck which would be the habit of that person just for owner change? "

Deven replies "Not really sure but it is my duty to say that person to transfer the ownership of it after sometime and after that, it totally depends on that person whether the person wants to be the depending person or the working person. "

Deven drinks water and one glass of water gives to Vivek and says "Wait a minute. "

He calls his sister, his sister receives and says "Tell me what you think about Vicky? "

Deven answers "Good man and above that really good person . By the way, I have called you to say that we are going somewhere we don't know, so it may take time. "

After thinking for three seconds, she says "O.k, take care, bye. "

Deven cuts the call and asks to Vivek "Let's try it, Are you ready? "

Vivek replies "Yes I am."

****